SYMPATHETIC MAGIC

A WITCHES OF CLEOPATRA HILL NOVEL

CHRISTINE POPE

DARK VALENTINE PRESS

SYMPATHETIC MAGIC

ISBN: 978-0692311462
Copyright © 2014 by Christine Pope
Published by Dark Valentine Press

Cover design and book layout by Indie Author Services.

To learn more about this author, go to
www.christinepope.com.

To everyone who ever dared to take a chance...

SYMPATHETIC MAGIC

CHAPTER ONE

MARGOT EMORY SLUNK OUT OF THE WEDDING RECEPTION and negotiated the rocky half-paved parking lot as best she could in her high-heeled sandals. All right, "slunk" probably wasn't the best word for it. Anyone looking at her would have probably said she was walking normally enough, aside from the occasional bobble when she hit a rock. No, it was more that she wished she could have crawled away, slithered out of there like the lizards that clung to the walls of her garden, because after that serious lapse in judgment, she didn't know if she could ever look any of the other McAllister witches in the face again.

What the hell were you thinking? she asked herself, sliding in behind the wheel of her Subaru, glad that at least it was dark so no one could see how her cheeks were burning. The proper response when a warlock from the Wilcox clan asked you to dance was, *Thank you, but no.*

That wasn't what had happened, though. When Lucas Wilcox approached her and extended a hand, she'd taken it like some simple-minded teenager dazzled that the popular boy had asked her to dance. And afterward, instead of coldly thanking him and marching off, dignity intact, she'd stammered some inane excuse about having to talk to the other McAllister elders and then had bolted like a frightened rabbit.

She rolled down the windows, wanting the fresh night breeze to blow through the car and help settle her roiling thoughts. Thank the Goddess that at least now, in mid-September, the evenings were cooling off enough that it made sense to rely on outdoor air rather than the A/C. Her cheeks still felt far too heated, though.

It must have been the champagne. She'd thought she'd been careful, had only drunk two narrow flutes' worth, but obviously that was too much for her to handle. Better to blame it on that than…well, on just about anything else.

All the way back to Jerome from the reception site in Sedona, Margot went over the scene in her mind, trying to decide if there really were a way she could have shot Lucas Wilcox down without making a scene. At the time she hadn't wanted to appear rude, not at Angela's wedding reception, not after everything the girl had gone through to get to her happy ending. Even after all that had happened, and so much had changed, Margot wasn't quite ready to accept the apparent truce that now existed between the two witch clans, no matter what the events of the past few months might have done to prove otherwise. When he approached her, she'd told herself that enduring a dance with Lucas Wilcox was better than refusing him and possibly causing him to press the issue.

And maybe he wouldn't have, she told herself. *Maybe he would've just accepted your refusal and gone to ask someone else to dance.*

Possibly, although even during their brief acquaintance, she'd learned he generally got his own way. Not rudely, not by forcing things, but somehow just…making them happen.

Which made sense, as that was his gift, after all. Lucky Lucas. The man for whom everything always magically went right. It was, as Angela had once remarked with a grin, a pretty damn good gift to have.

Except, of course, when it was working its magic on you. Then it didn't look like such a great gift after all.

Margot turned off 89A, using the short-cut through old town Cottonwood and and into

Clarkdale before getting back on the highway just as it curved around to head to Jerome, and up and over the mountain. By now it was getting late, almost eleven o'clock, although it appeared that she'd been one of the first to leave the reception.

Of course she had. Most of the clan members would stick around as long as the drink was flowing at the open bar…even Bryce, one of the other two elders. You'd think he'd know better. But the man had never met a whiskey on the rocks that he didn't like. Allegra Moss, the third clan elder, wasn't much of a drinker, but she also wouldn't pass up the chance to talk shop, as it were, with some of the Wilcox witches. Allegra always did like to pick people's brains.

The house felt empty, silent, when Margot entered and shut the front door behind her. No surprise there. Her mother had finally moved out a year earlier, declaring that she was tired of tripping over her daughter and wanted someplace where they wouldn't be in each other's laps. So she went down the hill to a "community for active seniors," to a house right on the fourteenth green of the golf course there.

"You don't play golf," Margot had pointed out, whereupon her mother grinned and said,

"No, but I like the green grass, and it's nice to have a house with a real right angle in it."

There wasn't much arguing with that point; buildings in Jerome had a tendency to sink and settle and shift in strange places, and the three-bedroom Victorian cottage where Margot had spent her entire life was no different. She couldn't even protest that a retirement community was no place for a self-respecting witch, not when a baker's dozen of McAllister witches and warlocks lived in the same development. In a way it made sense, as tiny Jerome couldn't really sustain the growing McAllister population, and so there were clan members down the hill in Clarkdale and Cottonwood, and over in Page Springs and Cornville, all the way down to Camp Verde by the freeway.

Even knowing all that, though, Margot still wasn't quite used to the stillness of the house now that her mother was gone. Worse, the cat who'd been their constant companion for the past seventeen years had passed on in early June, and though from time to time Margot had thought about replacing Felicity, she couldn't quite bring herself to do it.

Mouth thinning, she kicked off the high-heeled sandals that had been abusing her feet for the past six hours, then padded into the kitchen. Right now the best idea seemed to be brewing a cup of strong tea. Maybe then she could wash away the last of the champagne afterglow spinning around in her brain...and with it, wash away the memory of Lucas

Wilcox's arm around her waist, the strength of the shoulder under her hand…how good he had smelled.

All right, maybe *two* cups of tea.

"Was it something I said?" Lucas inquired of his cousin Connor, who had just gotten up from the table where he sat with Angela. Apparently he'd been heading over to inquire about the cake cutting, but he only made it a few feet before Lucas stopped him.

Connor's mouth worked; Lucas could tell he was fighting back a grin. "I don't know…what *did* you say to her?"

"Nothing much. In fact, I was so worried I'd end up offending her somehow that I didn't say anything for the whole song." He paused, his own mouth twisting. "Maybe that was the wrong approach. Maybe I should have said something about the weather or her dress or…well, *something*."

"Lucas, I have a feeling it isn't anything you said, or didn't say. Margot Emory's not exactly what I would call the friendly type." A lift of the shoulders, and Connor added, "If you wanted to make life difficult for yourself, you definitely chose the right person to chase after."

With that parting shot, he moved off in the direction of the resort's banquet manager, who was standing off to one side with a slightly glazed expression on his face. Probably trying to figure out how everything had gone so well, considering how quickly this entire affair had been put together. Lucas could have tried explaining that was his gift, that any enterprise he was involved with tended to go off without a hitch, but he had a feeling that would only make the manager's head explode…figuratively speaking, of course. No, better for him to simply think it was planning, planning, planning, and only a little bit of luck.

Lucas picked up a flute of champagne from the tray of a passing waiter and stared off in the direction of the parking lot, the direction where Margot had gone. It wouldn't be that hard to track her down; he knew she lived in Jerome, even if he didn't know the exact house. But if he drove up there now, he could allow his luck to guide him, and the odds were better than even that he'd end up parking his Porsche right in front of her place.

No, that was a terrible idea. She was already skittish as hell, and having him chase her up to her house would only make her go out and try to convince the other two McAllister elders that it was time to renew the anti-Wilcox wards that Angela had worked so hard to get removed from the little town's limits.

Elder. Lucas shook his head and took a healthy swallow of champagne. Even though he knew it was a title of authority and not one that was necessarily reflective of a given person's age, he found it difficult to apply that term to someone as lithe and lovely as Margot Emory. In fact, he'd gotten the impression that she was only a year or two younger than he, but she didn't look like someone closer to forty than twenty. He wondered how she did it.

Magic? Maybe. He knew she'd certainly cast a spell on him.

He finished the glass of champagne and contemplated snagging another. It wasn't as if he had to worry about driving, since he'd booked a room here at the resort. But he also didn't want to get stupid drunk, not at Connor and Angela's wedding reception. Half the McAllisters were giving him the side-eye already, and he knew he needed to behave himself.

So he grabbed a bottle of Perrier instead, then stood off on the sidelines as the happy couple headed to where the cake had been waiting in buttercream-frosted splendor this entire time, and went through the whole ritual of cutting the first piece and then feeding it to one another. Carefully, he noted— Angela had probably threatened Connor with some kind of whammy if he tried to smear cake all over her face. Then they went back to their seats, Angela moving a little slowly, as if her feet hurt. Poor kid. It was a long day for anyone, let alone a girl six months pregnant with twins.

When a waiter came up to offer Lucas a slice of the cake, he declined. He'd never had much of a sweet tooth. Anyway, he didn't want cake. He wanted Margot Emory.

It surprised him, the force of that desire. He'd never been the type to obsess over a woman. If she was interested, great, but if not, someone else was always bound to come along instead. Some irony, that the luck which made every other facet of his existence so easy clearly didn't work when it came to his love life. Sex life? Well, that was a different story. Sex was easy. But when he'd seen Margot for the first time last spring, at Connor's gallery opening—well, Lucas finally understood what people meant when they made comments about being hit by Cupid's arrow. He'd been struck, that was for damn sure.

More irony, that the woman he couldn't get out of his mind was probably the last one he should be interested in. She definitely didn't do anything to hide her dislike for the Wilcox clan and all it stood for, even though Connor and Angela were doing their damnedest to get people to understand that the clan was very different now that Connor was its leader, and not his brother Damon.

Well, it was certainly true that Damon hadn't done much to improve relations between the clans—the opposite, really. And while Lucas still mourned the loss of Connor's older brother, Lucas' own cousin and friend—the tragic waste of all that potential—he couldn't argue with that death. It had been necessary, and something Damon had brought on himself. Still, it hurt. Lucas had a lot of friends, but Damon had been one of the closest, despite their differences. And Damon…he'd been someone with many acquaintances, but only one or two he called "friend."

But Lucas didn't want to think about that now. Not here, at what should be a joyous occasion. He tried to tell himself that at least Margot had danced with him, hadn't thrown her drink in his face or said something particularly cutting or tried to hurl a fireball at him. Well, to be fair, he wasn't even sure she was capable of such a spell. He'd gathered from a few things Connor and Angela had said that Margot's talents lay in spells of illusion, not anything openly aggressive.

All right, so she'd danced with him. And then promptly bolted from the scene, as if she couldn't handle the realization that she'd allowed a Wilcox to manhandle her in front of all these people, many of them her own clan members. Her precipitous departure wasn't precisely a slap in the face, but it sure felt like it.

Lucas let out a sigh, then went in search of a waiter. It felt like time for that next glass of champagne after all.

Maybe it was because she'd tossed and turned for what seemed like half the night, but Margot overslept the next morning and then spent far too long taking a hot shower, as if by doing so she could wash away the last traces of Lucas Wilcox's touch. After she finished drying her hair, she belatedly recalled that she'd said she would check on the house for Angela, as Tobias and Rachel were still at the resort, remaining available to the staff there while the newlyweds departed for a tour of some of the wine-growing areas down in the south of the state. "A fact-finding mission," Angela had called it, no doubt referring to Connor's joint venture with a friend of theirs to open a new vineyard over in Page Springs.

Margot was sure the house was just fine, but Angela had been worried in all the hubbub that she hadn't locked up everything properly. Very well; Margot thought she'd hike up there after she had her usual tea and toast for breakfast, and rattle all the locks so she could say she'd done her duty. No one in the McAllister clan would disturb the place, and it was far enough off the beaten track that Margot somehow doubted a tourist would wander up there...especially with the illusions she'd set in place to prevent such a thing from happening…but it was a fine morning, and maybe the walk would help to clear her head a little.

The air did seem cooler today, a brisk breeze blowing from the northeast and pulling at a few stray tendrils of hair around her face. She let that wind guide her up the hill, a gentle pressure at her back, as if it were helping to propel her up the steep incline.

At the house, the front door was firmly locked, as she'd suspected. The back door that opened on the small garden and the path that led to the garage was not, however, and she shook her head at Angela's carelessness, even as she laid her hand on the door-knob and murmured the small charm that would make the tumblers turn and the door lock itself. Or maybe the unlocked door had been Connor's fault; Margot supposed a bride had a right to be a bit scat-terbrained on her wedding day, but Connor should have been paying better attention.

A crunch of gravel made her turn around, eyes narrowing. No one else should be up here, unless it was Connor and Angela coming back to Jerome for something they'd forgotten. But no, that didn't make sense. Margot knew the couple had planned to be on the road by around ten, and it was already almost eleven. They should be halfway to Phoenix by now.

The man who appeared around the corner of the house in that moment was tall and dark-haired, but he definitely was not Connor. He stopped a few feet away from where she stood on the back stoop, the expression in his eyes startled even behind the sunglasses he wore.

Despite her best efforts to ignore it, an odd little thrill traced its way down Margot's back. "What are you doing here, Lucas?"

At once he removed the sunglasses. His dark eyes twinkled in the bright sunlight. "Checking on the house. You?"

"The same," she said shortly. In that moment she wished she hadn't dressed so casually, that she wasn't wearing the skinny jeans she'd bought against her better judgment, the slim-fitting T-shirt, or the thong-style jeweled sandals that showed off her recent French pedicure. It was as if Lucas' gaze had caught every detail about her appearance, right down to her toes…and worse, he liked it.

At her reply, he let out a chuckle. "Those kids were so distracted, I think they probably forgot half of what they said to anyone over the past few days. Late last night, Connor asked me to come up and check on the house, since he was afraid he'd forgotten to lock the back door, and Rachel and Tobias were still going to be tied up at the resort today getting everything cleaned up and cleared out."

"Angela made the same request of me," Margot replied. "And good thing, since they actually did leave the back door unlocked. But I've taken care of it. Sorry you had to waste a drive out here."

"Oh, I don't think it was wasted," Lucas said, still with that glint in his eye.

The way he was looking at her left little doubt as to his meaning. She drew in a breath, trying to come up with a way to let him know there was no point in him wasting any more effort on her. Maybe in some small corner of her soul, she'd admit such attention was just the tiniest bit flattering, but her rational self knew she had to get rid of him now and offer nothing that could possibly be construed as encouragement. Goddess knows he was bad enough already when she was offering nothing but *dis*couragement.

He forestalled her, though, saying, "Well, since I'm here, why don't I buy you a drink?"

"A drink?" she repeated with some incredulity. "It's eleven o'clock in the morning."

"True," he said amiably. "But it's Sunday. Someone has to be offering brunch around here… you know…champagne? Mimosas?"

She crossed her arms and sent him what she hoped was a sufficiently quelling look. "This isn't your country club, Mr. Wilcox."

He did not appear offended. "Lucas. I'd say after that dance last night we should be on a first-name basis."

"Very well…Lucas." Although her tone was as severe as she could make it, his expression didn't change. He only stood there, gazing up at her where she stood on the back stoop, a slight smile playing about his mouth…a mouth she tried damn hard not to look at for very long. It was far too distracting. She went on, "No one offers brunch here in Jerome, and I don't generally make a habit of drinking before dinnertime."

"Okay, no mimosas. A cup of coffee?"

"Sorry, but I don't drink coffee."

"Iced tea? Sparkling water? Lemonade?"

Despite herself, Margot could feel her lips twitch. He was persistent, wasn't he? And after the last few fallow years, it felt good to have a man paying this much attention to her, even if the man in question happened to be a Wilcox.

But because he was a Wilcox, she knew she couldn't let that smile grow any further, couldn't do anything except send him on his way as soon as possible. Yes, Angela's constant message for the past few months had been Wilcox/McAllister togetherness, but Margot was not going to allow her *prima*'s wishes to sway her. Bad enough that Adam McAllister had been so openly flirting with that one Wilcox girl last night at the reception. So much for his supposedly broken heart. Margot knew she was made of sterner stuff.

"Nothing, thank you." She stepped down from the stoop, knowing she would have to go right past Lucas to make her escape. If only witches truly did have the ability to fly away on a broomstick. It would have been so much easier.

He did shift slightly on the path so she could walk past him, but not so much that she wasn't acutely aware of how tall he was, looming over her like that. Neither could she ignore the slightest tantalizing trace of the cologne he wore, something clean and woodsy, teasing her like a glimpse of the great pine forests surrounding Flagstaff itself, a place of course she'd never been.

"Rain check," he said, seeming content to stand there and watch her leave. A few more paces, and she'd made it past the corner of the house. Lucas was gone from her sight.

Why, then, did she experience a small pang, as if she wished he would have followed her?

CHAPTER TWO

LUCAS DROVE BACK TO FLAGSTAFF WITH THE TOP DOWN, letting the warm wind blow through his hair and wash over him. It was a beautiful mild mid-September day. The only thing that would have made it better would be to have Margot sitting in the passenger seat, less than a foot away from him. He could almost picture her there, a patterned scarf tied around her hair, sunglasses concealing her dark eyes. Very glamorous, very Audrey Hepburn.

Too bad there was probably a greater chance of the late Ms. Hepburn rising from the grave to ride with him than of Margot Emory ever condescending to do so.

The other times he had seen her, she'd been dressed conservatively and somewhat formally, in sheath dresses that complemented her slender frame but didn't exactly ooze sex appeal. Today, though, in those jeans, with the scoop neck of her T-shirt showing more cleavage than he'd expected and her pretty bare feet in those sandals?

In a word, damn.

Obviously Angela's determined *glasnost* policy of late hadn't done much to change Margot's opinion of any and all Wilcoxes, including himself. True, some walls took a long time to break down, but Ms. Emory's were obviously very thick. And high. And reinforced with steel, apparently.

Had she agreed to dance with him simply as a subtle way to torture him? Lure him into thinking she might be unbending a bit, just so she could go back to shooting him down unmercifully?

It might have been easier to think that, but for some reason Lucas didn't think it was precisely what was going on. More like…he'd caught her in an unguarded moment last night, and now she was doing whatever she could to recover the ground she thought she'd lost.

And it wasn't that she was seeing anyone else. Even before the reception, he'd gone back and forth as to whether he should just ask Angela about Margot, but when he'd actually worked up the nerve to call and do so, Angela wasn't home, and he didn't want to bother her by calling her cell when she was out and about…most likely occupied with some detail or other associated with planning the wedding, since that seemed to be her main reason for leaving the house, aside from her unending doctor's appointments. Of course, asking such questions of any of the other McAllisters was out of the question, so after some more hemming and hawing, he'd asked his friend Lester, the private investigator, to poke around a bit. Not a lot, not about anything that would be intrusive. Just to make sure Margot didn't have a boyfriend that she was keeping on the down-low.

There wasn't a lot to dig up, as it turned out. She'd been born at Verde Valley Medical Center, as were most of the McAllisters (those who weren't delivered by the clan healer back in the day, anyway), had gone to school in Clarkdale and Cottonwood. No record of any marriages. Mother lived down the hill in Clarkdale, father listed on the birth certificate as one Paolo Cantu but nowhere in evidence after that. Her name was on the deed to the house she lived in, a deed that had been updated about a year ago, when the mother relocated from Jerome to a senior community.

"Nothing besides that," Lester said, giving his report as the two of them shared a beer at the Beaver Street Brewery in downtown Flagstaff. "Not even a speeding ticket. Anyway, I hung around in Jerome for a few days, playing tourist, saw her come and go a bit. She had dinner with a couple of what looked like women friends one night. Drove down to Cottonwood to go to the grocery store. Spent a lot of time watering her roses. Sat in the garden and read a book, and then was writing in a notebook or something for a while." Lester shook his head, although his expression was amused, and took a swallow of beer. "A real pistol, that one."

Lucas had shot Lester a pained glance at that comment but decided to let it go.

Anyway, because of that bit of investigating, Lucas knew Margot was just as unattached as he. In a way, it would've been easier if she'd been seeing someone. Then he could blame her indifference on her unavailability, instead of her intractable inability to see that not every Wilcox was a black magic–wielding would-be kidnapper.

All right, Damon actually *had* been, but that was beside the point.

He didn't want to think about Damon, though. Right then he wished he didn't have to think about anything at all. It would be easier that way.

Forcing himself to focus on his surroundings, he saw that the scrub junipers flashing by had now given way to tall ponderosa pines. It still shocked him, the alteration in the landscape. How it happened so fast. A change in the elevation, he supposed.

He knew it was too much to hope that Margot's feelings toward him might shift that quickly.

The days went by quietly after that. Late in the week after their wedding, Angela and Connor returned to northern Arizona, spending a few days in the house on Paradise Lane before heading up to Flagstaff so they'd be there in time for her latest doctor's appointment. Angela seemed to have gotten visibly larger in only the few days they were away— or maybe it was just that Margot wasn't used to seeing her normally slender *prima* so, well, *round*.

"Everything okay with the house?" she asked of Margot. They were sitting on the front porch, enjoying a mild afternoon breeze, as the house was still somewhat warm.

"It was, after I checked. You did leave the back door unlocked."

Angela put a hand to her brow. "Oh, wow, sorry about that. But I guess it's good that I asked."

"Maybe, except that it was somewhat unnecessary, as Connor had asked the same thing of Lucas."

"He did?" she asked, her eyes widening. "Oops." Then she added, her expression growing somewhat sly, "And how is Lucas?"

"I wouldn't know," Margot said shortly, glad they were on the porch, so she could make a hasty escape.

"I haven't seen him since. I expect you'll find out when you go back to Flagstaff."

And after that she said a quick farewell and departed, inwardly fuming. Had it been a simple mistake…or had Connor and Angela both asked their respective relatives to come check on the house so they'd "accidentally" bump into each other?

Goddess save her from happy couples who felt the need to matchmake every unattached individual in a ten-mile radius.

By the time Margot got back to her house, she could practically feel the scowl she'd dug into her own forehead—a scowl that didn't lessen when she saw that her mother's car was parked behind hers in the driveway. True, because of the way the lot was set up, there really wasn't anyplace else to park, but really, the last person she felt like talking to now was Sylvia Emory.

I knew I should've gotten the key back from her, Margot thought in annoyance, although she knew locked doors didn't stop most witches if they wanted to get in. Still, whatever happened to privacy?

She did her best to settle her expression in more serene lines as she entered the house. The smell of cinnamon tea drifted out to her. Normally, it was a scent she enjoyed, one that evoked changing leaves and colder days and the Halloween decorations nearly everyone in Jerome put up. Now, though, it just told her that her mother had gone ahead and made herself at home in the kitchen.

Attempting not to sigh, Margot entered that room, saw her mother sitting at the round table under the window, watching the late afternoon sunlight slant in through the stained-glass suncatcher hanging there, casting hues of blue and red and gold and green over the white tile countertops.

"Tea?" said her mother, lifting a chubby brown teapot from the trivet that sat in the middle of the table.

"Thank you," Margot replied. She knew it was pointless to ask her mother what she wanted, or what she was doing there. In time she'd get around to it, but on her own terms.

"I see our *prima* is back in town," Sylvia remarked. "Not staying, though, I would imagine."

"Not for long." After blowing on her tea, feeling her mother's sharp blue gaze on her, Margot added, "She has to see the doctor soon."

"And I imagine she'd rather be someplace cooler. What were those two thinking, going all the way down to Bisbee in September? It must have been a hundred degrees."

"They wanted to see the vineyards, talk to the growers." Yes, there were vines planted all over the Verde Valley, but the growers still got a good portion of their grapes from the wine-growing regions down south, especially around Willcox. Margot tried not to think of the irony of that one small town being given that name. Two "L"s, to be sure, but still….

"Hmm," her mother said, which could have meant anything. Really, why was she here? It wasn't out of character for her to drop by unexpectedly, but in general she only did that when they hadn't seen each other for a few weeks. Since not even a week had passed since the wedding, and Margot had shared a table with her mother then, she couldn't quite figure out why the urgent need to be here now, of all days.

"And what have you been up to?" Sylvia asked then.

Something seemed to click in Margot's head. She set down her teacup, shot her mother a narrow look, and replied, "Nothing at all. Tending my garden. Reading. Renewing the illusion across Boyd Willis's driveway again so another drunk tourist won't back into his garage."

That driveway had proved to be a magnet to intoxicated or merely befuddled travelers over the years…until Margot came up with the idea to cast a long-lasting illusion of a sturdy stone wall across the entrance to his property. Even someone who'd spent a hard afternoon drinking at the Spirit Room tended to look twice before backing into that. But the spell wouldn't hold indefinitely, so she main-tained a schedule of refreshing it every two weeks.

The only drawback was that Boyd had to wait until the street was absolutely empty of civilians before he came and went, as otherwise they would see him backing his ancient F-150 right through a wall, but that seemed a small price to pay compared to having to replace the garage door once a year.

"That's all?" her mother asked.

Irritated, Margot snapped, "What else would I be doing?"

Without blinking, Sylvia reached out and poured some more tea into her cup. The sweet-smelling tendrils of steam curled upward, and she inhaled deeply, then said, "Well, I'd hoped you might be getting out and about more."

"And where precisely am I supposed to be getting out and about? I'm an elder here—I can't just go running around on a whim."

Her mother looped a finger into the handle of her teacup but didn't lift it, seeming content to merely let it rest there on the tabletop. "I think you could go many places, if you'd only allow yourself."

"And what precisely is that supposed to mean?" Her mother loved to talk that way, in elliptical sentences that made her sound like the clan seer. In reality, her gift was for growing things—the glory of the garden outside was her work originally, although Margot privately thought she did just fine on her own without any magical help.

"My dear, the borders are open! We can go almost anywhere we like now. Haven't you ever wanted to see Flagstaff?"

"No," Margot said shortly. That was a lie, as she'd often wondered when she was younger what it would be like to walk amongst those ponderosa forests, to breathe in cool air scented with pine. Those lands had been off limits for so many years that she'd stopped thinking about them somewhere along the line. Now, though, with this new joining of the clans, she realized she could go there…if she dared.

Her mother lifted an eyebrow and finally took a sip of her tea. "Not even to see your new friend?"

"Friend?" Margot asked, although she thought she knew exactly who her mother was talking about.

"The tall one…you know…who you danced with at the reception."

More than ever she found herself regretting that single foolish lapse in judgment. It seemed everyone was conspiring to get her together with Lucas Wilcox. Well, all right, not everyone—she had no doubt that Bryce McAllister and Allegra Moss would be properly horrified if hers and Lucas' "relationship," if one could call it that, were to progress any further than that one ill-advised dance.

"If you mean Lucas Wilcox," Margot said, not bothering to hide the irritation in her voice, "he is not my 'friend,' and I have no intention of going to Flagstaff to see him, or for any other reason."

"Too bad," her mother replied, her placid expression saying that she was used by now to her daughter's curtness. "He's a handsome one."

"He's a Wilcox."

"So? Being with a Wilcox seems to be working fairly well for our *prima*."

This was ridiculous. Connor's and Angela's was a very special case, a relationship that apparently had been preordained by the Goddess. Margot wouldn't question the situation, as it was clear they were meant to be together, but one fated pairing didn't mean it was suddenly open season on all the Wilcox men. Maybe her mother could forget how Damon Wilcox had kidnapped Angela right from her bedroom, and how his grandfather had attempted to do the same thing with Aunt Ruby back in the day, but Margot's own memory wasn't quite so short. Yes, according to Angela, Lucas had nothing to do with Damon's plots, had actually tried to talk him out of the kidnapping, but that didn't change the fact that he was born a Wilcox, was still a Wilcox, and would be a Wilcox until the day he died.

Just as she was a McAllister. Oh, her last name was Emory, but her grandmother had been Amanda McAllister, and so Margot was as much a part of the clan as anyone. More so, as she was an elder. And a

McAllister elder couldn't go off dallying with one of the Wilcoxes, no matter how good-looking he might be.

And that, she thought, *is a big part of the problem. Those Wilcox men…they definitely have the "tall, dark, and handsome" thing down pat. I doubt they'd be as much trouble if they didn't.*

"Mother, if you've only come up here to ask whether I'm seeing Lucas Wilcox, the short answer is no, I'm not, and the slightly longer answer is, no, I am not, and never will."

For a few seconds her mother didn't say anything, only drummed her fingers against the glazed ceramic surface of the teacup she held. At last she said, her tone far gentler than her daughter's, "Margot, being an elder doesn't mean you have to live your life alone. That's not what anyone intended."

Oh, why was it that mothers always knew the exact wrong thing to say? Even after all these years, the hurt stirred within her, waking memories she'd worked far too hard to put away. "Maybe that's not what they intended," she said shortly. "But that seems to be how it's working out."

Before Lucas knew it, October arrived, and with it the first gusts of colder air. People on the streets started wearing jackets and boots. One morning he looked out his kitchen window and saw frost on the grass, and realized the first snows of late autumn might only be a month away.

He thought he'd done a good job of trying to forget about Margot. There were days of golf with his friends while the trees around them shifted into brilliant shades of gold and red and orange. He puttered in the garden, had dinner at Connor and Angela's house—that girl definitely knew how to cook—read the financial papers and waited for the twinge that would tell him which stocks to buy and which to sell. In between, he sometimes went out to the bars and restaurants in downtown Flagstaff. He met women there, women who were pretty clear about their interest in him. The only difference was, now he found he really wasn't interested in them. One or two he took out to dinner, then realized there was no point in going any further than that. He'd been down that road before, tried dating civilians, tried seeing a few of his more distant cousins. None of it worked. His love life was where his luck invariably failed him.

Mornings like this one, though…he couldn't help wondering what it would be like to have Margot here next to him, making tea—he preferred coffee, but he'd make that sacrifice for her—planning a walk in the woods to enjoy the last of the autumn colors… experiencing the afterglow of early-morning sex.

Ha. Considering she'd barely look him in the eye, getting from there to making love was sort of a jump. Never mind that he hadn't seen her for more than a month. Now, Halloween was just a little more than a week away.

Halloween....

Lucas pondered that thought for a moment. He knew Connor had first seen Angela in person at the Jerome Halloween dance, his identity as a warlock carefully concealed by one of Damon's clever spells. There was no stricture against Wilcox clan members going now—in fact, he'd heard that Mason was plan-ning to attend, as she and Adam McAllister had been conducting a long-distance relationship over the past month. Her parents were not all that happy about the situation, and his apparently even less so, but the couple seemed to be following Angela's lead in say-ing the inter-clan feud was over.

So, great for them. What was he thinking, that he could just go down there and hope lightning would strike for him the way it had for Connor and Angela? History didn't tend to repeat itself that way. Besides, he had no idea if Margot was even going. She didn't exactly seem like the Halloween costume type when you got right down to it. Then again, the dance was a Jerome institution, and from what he'd heard, the elders did go to show their support.

Well, that clinched it. He only had a few days to figure out what he'd wear, and maybe he'd end up looking like an idiot, but he wasn't going to pass up an opportunity to face Margot Emory on her home turf.

Was there ever a witch with less enthusiasm for Halloween? Margot wondered, and frowned at her reflection. Yes, it was traditional that all the elders go to the dance, but she didn't quite see the point. It wasn't as if it were a McAllister function, not really; the dance was put on as a fundraiser by the volunteer fire department, about half of whom were civilians. But she'd given up trying to get out of it.

She smoothed her long skirt, then reached up to adjust the golden circlet she wore on her head. If she had to go to this thing, then she'd go looking dignified, which was why for the past few years she'd dressed up as Eleanor of Aquitaine, in a flowing medieval gown with a jeweled belt and a crown and veil, her long dark hair lying loose over her shoulders. All right, apparently Eleanor had been a strawberry blonde, but Margot somehow doubted most people attending the Jerome Halloween dance were that dedicated to historical accuracy.

A glance at the clock told her it was already almost eight. The dance was always full to capacity, but she knew she didn't have to worry about getting in, nor having no place to sit once she got there. The elders always had a table reserved for them, and for whichever family members they decided to favor by allowing them to sit in the empty seats.

It was a cool night, with a brisk wind blowing from the east. Over the Mogollon Rim, a horizontal half moon, the one sometimes called the "witch's cup," had begun to rise. Margot allowed herself a brief glance at it, then continued to walk steadily toward Spook Hall, where the dance was always held. Another good thing about this costume—she could wear flat ballet-style slippers with it. Much better for negotiating Jerome's slanted and uneven sidewalks than the heels some women forced themselves into for the event.

As always, she ducked in through the side entrance, avoiding the queue at the front. Matt McAllister, one of Jerome's volunteer firemen, was standing guard duty at that door to prevent people from doing the very thing she had just done, but of course he merely waved her through, saying, "Your table's in the same place, Margot."

Of course it was. And it would be the same people sitting at it, just as they always did, year after year. Well, except last year. Then it had been Angela's contingent of "bodyguards," of whom Margot had been one. Fat lot of good that had done. It still wasn't easy to admit that Damon Wilcox had managed to slip his own brother into this event, right in the very heart of McAllister territory. Even now she couldn't help wondering if there was something she could have done to detect Damon's spell, although logically she knew that merely being able to cast illusions didn't necessarily mean you could see through those created by someone else.

She repressed a sigh and pushed through the expanding crowd to the table where Allegra and Bryce were already seated. Allegra's husband sat next to her in one of the spare seats, and Bryce's wife beside him. That left three extras, after Margot claimed hers, and she always let Allegra and Bryce hand those off to those of their children who might need them. It wasn't as if Margot ever brought a date.

A date. There was a good one.

Luckily, it was dark enough in the room that she doubted the others could see the sour expression she currently wore, although she did her best to remove it before she sat down. "Evening," she said, nodding at the group, all of whom had drinks in front of them already.

"Happy Halloween!" chirped Allegra, and Margot felt the scowl begin to creep back. Samhain itself wasn't for another three days, after all, and it should mean something quite different to the witches in her clan than it did all the civilians around them. It was a time for acknowledging the change of the seasons, and those who had gone before them, not for dressing up and looking for any excuse to attend a party.

She managed a faint smile and sat down, then realized she probably should have gone to get a drink first. Not that she ever drank much at these things. Still, something told her this was one night where getting mildly intoxicated might not be such a bad idea. It wasn't as if she had to worry about driving home.

In the meantime, there were bottles of water sitting in the middle of the table, so she reached over and took one.

"A good turnout tonight," Allegra said, her voice pitched unnaturally loud to carry over the music. At the moment it was a recording; the band wouldn't start playing for another fifteen minutes or so.

Since that was the same thing Allegra said almost every year, Margot summoned another half-hearted smile and nodded, but didn't bother to reply. Obviously used to this sort of behavior, Allegra gave a slight shrug and turned back to her husband, continuing the conversation they'd been holding as to whether having ten pumpkins was enough for Halloween, or whether they should go get some more.

As if it matters, Margot thought. Yes, there were a score of McAllister children in Jerome young enough to care about trick-or-treating, but she thought they probably cared a good deal more about the type of candy the Moss household would be handing out rather than how many pumpkins decorated the front porch of their somewhat ramshackle Victorian house.

She drank some water and gazed out at the crowd. The room already seemed filled to bursting, so fairly soon they would start turning people away at the door. Where those disappointed attendees would go, she had no idea. Possibly there were other Halloween parties down in Cottonwood. She'd never paid much attention to the existence of any alternatives, as of course she always had a place here.

The band started up, roaring into a spirited rendition of "Monster Mash," and Margot let out a sigh. Same music, different year. It wasn't even that she disliked loud music, although she was sure most people who knew her would be surprised by that. No doubt she looked to them like the type who would have Mozart playing in the background all day. Little did they know that sometimes she'd close all the windows and shut the blinds, and blast the music she'd loved back in high school, Pearl Jam and Nirvana and Green Day, singing along as she dusted and watered her plants. What was that saying? "Dance like nobody's watching"?

No, it was just that it was *always* the same music at these things. Not in the same order, necessarily, but even when the band tried to mix things up, it all had a depressing sameness. Then again, how many Halloween-themed songs were there?

As she watched, Adam McAllister led Mason Wilcox out onto the dance floor, he in a cowboy getup she thought he'd worn last year, too, she in a fanciful Indian maiden dress with her long dark hair in two braids. So much for cultural appropriation, although Margot supposed Mason had more claim to it than some, considering how many members of the Wilcox family had some amount of Navajo blood.

Speak of the devil. Two tables over she saw Angela and Connor, her friend Sydney and Sydney's fiancé, Anthony, and sitting opposite them, Angela's father and his new—well, they weren't married, and Margot didn't know if they planned to be, but it seemed fairly clear that Andre Wilcox or Begonie or whatever he was calling himself these days and Marie Wilcox, his significant other, were pretty serious about each other. In fact, Andre was taking Marie's hand and leading her out to the dance floor, and she was laughing, actually laughing. Margot had spent too much time wearing a less-than-pleasant expression on her face not to recognize that history in someone else's features, but even so, Andre seemed enchanted by Marie.

In fact, just about everywhere she looked, she saw people paired off—the other elders and their spouses, Adam and Mason, Connor solicitously bringing Angela a bottle of water, since she was so big now that trying to navigate the crowded room would have been even more of a chore than usual. Even sour-faced Marie wasn't alone. Not that she looked particularly sour-faced at the moment.

And then it all felt to be too much, and Margot set down her own bottle of water and stood.

"Going somewhere?" Bryce inquired.

"I just need some fresh air," she replied, voice sounding strangled even to herself.

She pushed through the ranks of people who weren't dancing, heading out the front door with no place particular in mind, as long as she didn't have to stay inside. Half a block up the street was the Cellar 433 wine-tasting room, and as they weren't currently open, she guessed they wouldn't mind if she sat on their front steps for a few minutes to clear her head.

Immediately outside Spook Hall, the sidewalk was nearly as crowded as it was inside, but once she got past those clots of people smoking or just chatting, the area was clear. No point in any of them going where she was headed, with the business closed for the evening.

The steps to Cellar 433 were low and wide, but a bench she'd forgotten about had been placed in front of one of the windows, so she took a seat there, then breathed in some of the cool night air, trying to compose herself. Really, she didn't know what had gotten into her lately. It wasn't as if she hadn't had plenty of time to get used to her solitary existence. Certainly it had never bothered her much before this.

And she did not want to be one of those hateful people who begrudged others their happiness. Connor and Angela had certainly earned theirs, and Marie and Andre, too, if what Margot had heard was true. No, she was probably just tired. Tired of doing what everyone expected of her. Tired of thinking ahead and realizing that every year was going to be more or less like this one, right up to the day she died and someone else took her position as elder.

If you came out here to try to cheer yourself up, you're not exactly going about it the right way, she told herself. *Try to get your wits together, for the Goddess' sake!*

A flash of white approaching her took her by surprise, and she blinked. For the barest second, she thought maybe she was seeing one of Angela's ghosts, then realized the white was simply a dinner jacket. The man wearing it stopped at the bottom of the steps and smiled up at her.

"Hello, Margot," said Lucas Wilcox.

CHAPTER THREE

THE LAST THING LUCAS HAD COUNTED ON WAS DRIVING all the way down here to Jerome, only to be turned away at the door to the hall where the Halloween dance was being held.

"Sorry, man," said the kid at the door, who was wearing an old-fashioned black and white striped prison uniform. "We were sold out by eight-thirty. Better luck next year."

Luck. There was a joke. His much-vaunted luck hadn't helped him out much in this situation.

It passed briefly through his mind to try pulling a Damon, to rise to his full height and demand, "Do you know who I am?" But this was probably the last place in the world a trick like that would work, and so he'd only muttered, "It's fine," and then moved a few paces away from the building so he could gather his thoughts.

Turning around and going straight back to Flagstaff seemed anticlimactic at best. Well, he'd passed a bar as he walked down here. Maybe he should go in and have one pity drink, then head home. He couldn't think of what else to do with himself.

As he climbed back up the hill, though, he saw the slightest movement in the shadows in front of a small building at the end of the street, right before the place where he'd turn to go up toward the bar and the spot where his car was parked. Something glittered there in the darkness, and as his eyes focused, he realized it was a woman wearing a regal-looking costume, a circlet studded with paste gems on her head. And then he looked closer, and realized it was Margot Emory.

What she might be doing sitting out here, he couldn't begin to guess, although if it was really that crowded inside, he could see why she'd want to make her escape to someplace a little quieter. He approached, and greeted her. She started, looking as if she'd seen a ghost—not that strange in Jerome, he supposed—then tried to cover up her reaction by giving him a sardonic smile.

"You do turn up in the oddest places," she said. "What in the world are you doing here?"

"I thought I was going to a dance," he replied, jerking a thumb down the street in the direction of the hall. What did they call the building? Spook Hall.

Crazy.

"So they're already turning people away? You should've gotten here earlier."

"Well, this is my first time at one of these things," he replied, and wished he'd kept his mouth shut. The comment only seemed to point out that, up until recently, the Wilcoxes had been *persona non grata* in Jerome.

She got up from where she'd been sitting, moving out where he could see her more clearly. Now he could tell that the gown she wore was dark crimson velvet, with a jeweled belt clasped around her slender waist. Her inky hair lay loose over her shoulders under the long white veil that covered her head, and she was positively breathtaking.

Somehow he managed to find his breath, despite that. "Well, since I'm shut out, and it doesn't look like you're too interested in being there, why don't we go up the street, and I'll finally buy you that drink? It's definitely not eleven o'clock on a Sunday morning."

Her mouth opened, and he tensed, waiting for the inevitable refusal. Her next words surprised him. "What on earth are you wearing? This is a Halloween party, not a wedding."

He straightened the white dinner jacket. "I couldn't think of what to wear. I'll admit this would've worked better if I could've gotten inside and ordered a martini."

"Shaken, not stirred?"

"Exactly," he said, relieved that she hadn't yet shot him down, and shocked that she'd gotten the James Bond reference. For some reason, he'd gotten the impression that the witches of Cleopatra Hill tended to be a bit detached from popular culture.

"Well," she said, and hesitated. It almost looked as if she was debating with herself, attempting to decide what she should do next. Then she smiled at him, a smile with no irony or sarcasm in it. The expression brightened her face so much that he could only stare at her, wondering what on earth she was about to say.

"Well," she went on, and her voice sounded firmer this time, "if we go up to the Spirit Room, I'm pretty sure the bartender can get you that martini."

Temporary insanity?

Maybe.

She sat with Lucas in one of the high booths at the back of the bar, a place where they were guaranteed a bit more privacy than if they'd taken one of the tables toward the front, and definitely more than if they'd sat at the bar itself. Thank the Goddess that the bartender on duty tonight was a civilian, and not one of her many McAllister cousins. Word would still get out that she'd been seen in here with a strange man, but at least it would take a little longer for the gossip to get through the family grapevine. What the bartender—or the few other civilians in here—thought of a medieval queen sitting down with a man who looked like a refugee from the set of *Casablanca*, she didn't know. Then again, it was close to Halloween, and the dance was going on around the corner.

Oh, who was she kidding? No one in Jerome would have batted an eye at what they were wearing, no matter what time of year it was.

When he'd asked her what she wanted to drink, she hesitated. Considering the circumstances, it probably would've been wisest to order something very light, like a white wine spritzer. Never mind that that wasn't the sort of drink people generally ordered at the Spirit Room.

"Jack and Coke," she'd said recklessly, and Lucas' right eyebrow lifted so much that he really did look a bit like Sean Connery for a split second.

But he'd gotten the drink without further comment, along with his own martini, and brought both drinks back to the booth where she waited. When she sipped at her J&C, as they'd used to call them back in the day, it recalled to mind those times when she and her friends would sneak the booze out of their parents' liquor cabinets, then take their cans of "Coke" with them when they went to hang out in various backyards during the long, lazy days of summer, not thinking about anything much except their next ramble down to the river, or maybe who was seeing whom and whether any of those romances would last past high school. Back then she'd certainly never thought she'd be approaching forty with not even a cat for company.

"You're very far away," Lucas said, and she snapped her attention back to the here and now, to the somewhat overwhelming presence of the man who sat next to her.

"Sorry," she replied at once. "I haven't had one of these in a while."

"And it has that much of an effect on you? You've only had two sips."

Despite herself, she grinned. "No, not that. We used to drink these in high school. Guess it just took me back."

He was watching her closely, dark eyes intent. Another of those not entirely unwelcome shivers worked its way down her back. "I have a hard time imagining you doing anything that…illicit."

"Oh, we all had our rebellious stages, I guess," she told him. "I got over mine pretty quickly, though."

"Apparently."

An awkward silence descended, while she sipped again at her Jack and Coke, and he took a slightly larger swallow of his martini. Vodka, she thought, judging by the smell, not gin. As if it mattered.

"I'd expected this place to be more crowded," Lucas commented then, gesturing with his free hand toward the rest of the bar and the random half-dozen or so patrons it currently boasted.

Glad of the chance to move on to a more neutral topic, Margot replied, "It will be later. Right now the dance is just getting started. Once the band has done a few sets and they've announced the winners of the costume contest, people will start to trickle in here. I've heard it can get pretty packed."

"Then I'm glad we got here early." His gaze was warm as he looked at her, and she was uncomfortably aware of just how close he sat, so close she could once again catch the faintest trace of the cologne he wore. She could see how thick his dark eyelashes were, the faint brush of gray at his temples.

A warmth began in the pit of her stomach that didn't have much to do with the whiskey she'd just consumed, and she looked away, pretending to gaze at the painting over the bar, the coffered ceiling, so lovingly restored. *I shouldn't have come here,* she thought then, but couldn't summon the will to extricate herself. It would be terribly rude to run out on him now.

And...she really didn't want to.

What *did* she want? More to the point, what did *he* want?

She wasn't sure she wanted to know the answer to either of those questions.

Clearing her throat, she asked, "So, Lucas, what do you Wilcoxes do on Samhain? Any particular observances?" *Oh, Goddess, that sounded terrible. And judgmental…"you Wilcoxes," indeed.*

If he saw anything wrong with the question, he didn't show it. "We're not really practitioners of the old ways like you are here in Jerome," he said easily. "We have our solstice observations, but that's about it. In Flagstaff, Samhain is just Halloween. The clan members with kids that age will be taking them trick-or-treating, I suppose."

"Oh," she said, her tone sounding flat. "Then I suppose Connor will be here with us?"

"I would assume so. If Angela's up to—well, whatever it is you do."

There was just the slightest hint of a question in his words. "Nothing taxing. The *prima* decides on the particulars of the ceremony, so I have no doubt Angela will tailor it to her…condition."

Lucas nodded but didn't reply, instead taking another swallow of his martini. Was he wondering if she would invite him? No, that was ridiculous. Have a Wilcox present at one of their most sacred rites?

Well, Connor is going to be there, and he's a Wilcox….

She shoved the thought out of her head. "I fear that's the last we'll have of her for a while, because the doctor doesn't want her that far away as she gets closer to her due date. So much for summering in Flagstaff and wintering here in Jerome."

"Well, there are extenuating circumstances on this go-round," Lucas said, his tone so gentle that she couldn't take it as a rebuke. Well, mostly. "I'm sure next year things will be on a more or less regular schedule."

As regular as it could be with twins. Margot tried to imagine caring for two infants at the same time, but as she was an only child, her imagination rather failed her on that point. The prospect seemed somewhat horrifying to her, but Angela and Connor appeared to regard raising twins as their next great adventure together.

"I'm sure," she echoed in absent tones, wondering where she would be a year from now. Here, naturally. Well, not here at the Spirit Room, but down the street at Spook Hall, listening to the same music, watching the same couples get up and dance. Would Adam and his new Wilcox girlfriend be married by then?

Probably, considering the way these things have been going lately, she thought drearily, and then wondered why that prospect sounded so depressing.

"Hey," said Lucas, and Margot looked up from her drink to see him studying her, dark brows pulled together in a worried frown.

"What?"

"A woman dressed as a medieval queen and drinking a Jack and Coke should look a little happier than you do."

"Well," Margot replied, attempting to shake off the dark mood, "I *am* dressed as Eleanor of Aquitaine. From what I can recall, she had quite a bit on her plate."

A chuckle. "My history's a little rusty, so I'll take your word for it. But…you do seem a little down."

Now was the time when she should tell him that how she felt was none of his business. And really, it wasn't. But…were her feelings written that clearly on her face, even after all the efforts she'd made over the years to cultivate what she hoped was a serene expression that revealed nothing of what might be going on inside?

Her mouth opened, but instead of letting out the retort she'd planned, she asked, "Do you ever get tired, Lucas?"

"Tired?" he repeated, lifting an eyebrow. "In general, or of something in particular?"

"I don't know," she said, regretting that she'd ever allowed such an ill-considered remark to escape her mouth. "Of doing what you're supposed to do."

At her words, he gave the faintest of nods, then lifted his martini and took a contemplative swallow.

"I have a feeling most people do. But it doesn't have to be that way."

Margot drank some of her J&C before replying, "It doesn't?" At the same time she thought, *Maybe it doesn't have to be that way for you, because you seem like someone who gets what he wants without even having to try.*

To her surprise, his expression darkened, and he set down his glass, running a finger down the stem as he appeared to measure what he was going to say next. "People think I have it easy because of my gift. But that's not really true."

"Oh, come on," she said. "Don't try to tell me it's some kind of curse to always have everything go right in everything you do."

"But that's just the problem."

She widened her eyes at him, and he went on,

"People think everything works out perfectly for me, that nothing has ever gone wrong in my life, but that's not the case."

"I find that hard to believe." *Sorry, Lucas, but there's only room for one at this pity party. And no one's going to attend one thrown for a handsome, rich, successful warlock....*

The heavy lashes dropped, and in that moment it seemed as if the lines around his eyes were deeper than they'd been a few seconds ago. "I'm alone, aren't I?"

He'd spoken the words simply, with no attempt at pathos, but she sensed it in him, an echo of the same emptiness she felt. An odd, brief moment of vulnerability, when, from what she'd seen of him, he was the one in the room with the sunniest smile, the ready quip, the air of infinite possibilities. Was that all a façade?

Margot wasn't sure how she should feel about that. Despite her best efforts to control it, a wave of pity went over her. No, that wasn't quite right. Not pity, exactly.

Understanding.

But things had gotten intimate way too quickly. She didn't want to go there yet. *Ever*, she told herself. *You don't ever want to go there. Not with Lucas Wilcox.*

After sipping at her J&C again, and realizing it was disappearing far more quickly than she'd intended, she said in a purposely light tone, "Well, how alone can any of us be when we're surrounded by clan members day and night?"

His expression shifted abruptly at her words, and the easy smile she remembered first seeing across Angela's dining room table touched his mouth. "That's for damn sure. At least in Flagstaff we're sort of spread out. I don't know how you do it, all jammed together here in Jerome."

The moment had been lost. For a second or two, Margot regretted her words, regretted being so much of a coward that she couldn't even handle a minute or two of honest communication with him. But no, it was better this way. Keep it light, and maybe he'd forget how they'd both started to open up to one another.

"Oh, we're not all here, Lucas. We have quite a contingent down in Clarkdale and Cottonwood, and also in Camp Verde. There's even a small colony over in Prescott." Damn. Why had she brought up Prescott? Most of the time, she did a pretty good job of pretending the town didn't exist. She didn't want to think about Prescott…didn't want to think about *him*.

She must have gotten her mask more or less back in place, though, since Lucas didn't seem to notice anything strange in her expression or tone. "That's true," he said. "I guess I just associate you McAllisters so much with this crazy little town that I forget you've spread out a good deal."

"Not much of a choice there," she replied. "As you might have noticed, there isn't what you'd call much undeveloped land around here. We had to go somewhere."

"Well, I shouldn't really be one to talk. The Wilcox clan isn't exactly confined to Flagstaff, either."

The conversation wended its way to safer topics then, as they talked about the places they'd been and seen, and the work involved in keeping the nature of their families' talents hidden from the outside world. Somewhere in the middle of that conversation, both their drinks ran out, and Lucas got up to fetch them another round. Margot wasn't sure how good an idea that was, but since he'd managed to slip out of the booth and get halfway to the bar before she could summon the will to protest, she decided to let it go. After all, the drinks weren't that strong. She felt barely swimmy. A second one shouldn't be too much to handle.

A few more people had trickled in during the past quarter-hour or so, and she couldn't help noticing how the women in the bar watched Lucas' progress, some of their stares downright predatory. All right, if she allowed herself to look at him objectively, forget that he was a Wilcox, then yes, she had to admit that he was a very handsome man.

Oh, who are you kidding? she thought. *He's probably the best-looking man you've ever seen.* Not that it really made much of a difference one way or another. So he was gorgeous. He was also severely off-limits.

Seemingly unaware of the way the women's attention tracked him back to the booth, Lucas slid in next to Margot and set a fresh Jack and Coke in front of her. As he did so, several groups of people entered the room and headed straight for the bar.

"Looks like I made it back in the nick of time," he remarked, raising his martini toward hers in a mock salute. "Is the dance over already?"

She never wore a watch, but Lucas' was visible enough. Something slim and probably hideously expensive, although she didn't know the brand. "Not at barely nine o'clock," she replied after taking a quick glance at the time. "The band must be taking a break. I think some people come up here for a drink because it's faster than waiting in line at the dance."

"Makes sense."

He drank, and since she didn't know what else to do, Margot sipped at her J&C and barely avoided a wince. Damn. It tasted as if the bartender had reversed the ratio of Jack to Coke on this go-round. But she didn't want to make a scene by sending it back, especially since she had a feeling Lucas would try to tease her about not holding her liquor if she protested that the drink was too strong. No, she'd just have to take very small sips and hope he wouldn't notice that she was taking her time with this round.

Despite her caution, she could feel the whiskey hitting her, bringing with it a not entirely unpleasant sensation of lightheadedness. When was the last time she'd gotten tipsy? She honestly couldn't remember. Not at Angela and Connor's wedding. No, she'd been sober enough then, even though she'd wanted to blame her insanity in dancing with

Lucas on being too drunk to know what she was doing. Unfortunately, a glass and a half of champagne wasn't even enough to make her tipsy, let alone drunk.

Now, though....

She wished she'd asked him to bring her some water. Her throat suddenly felt dry, and wetting it too deeply with the concoction before her brought its own risks.

"...doing next Friday?"

"What?" she asked, blinking. Damn, once again she'd been off in the clouds and hadn't heard what he said.

Lucas gave her a curious look, but only said, "Next week is the first Friday art walk in Sedona. I was asking if you were doing anything next Friday."

The truthful answer was that no, she wasn't doing anything at all...or at least nothing she hadn't done thousands of times before. Puttering in the garden and maybe doing some sketches of the fall foliage, tidying the house, walking over Jerome to make sure all the subtle little illusions she'd set out were still there and doing their job of pointing the tourists and any other outsiders away from places the local witches didn't want them going. It was a great way to keep in shape, that was for sure, hiking up and down all those steep, narrow streets. However, it certainly wasn't anything she absolutely had to do that day.

She hesitated for a long time. The question had been phrased in the gentlest of ways, but Lucas was still basically asking her out on a date. She couldn't go on a date with him. Totally out of the question.

"I have a lot I need to do here, actually," she said, and took a fortifying sip of her Jack and Coke so she wouldn't have to see his reaction.

"Connor's going to have some new pieces at Red Rock Illuminations. He can't really do a big opening right now, what with Angela needing to stay in Flagstaff after Samhain, but these are paintings no one's seen before. I think it would mean a lot to him if there were some family members there to support him."

Oh, very clever. Couch it as doing something for Connor, rather than going out on a real date. "I—"

"It'll be fun." Lucas was holding his martini glass but not lifting it to his lips. Instead, he kept his gaze fixed on her, even as his mouth quirked. "You know, *fun?* Remember what that is?"

"I'm well aware of the concept," she snapped.

He didn't reply, but his gaze clearly said, *Are you?*

"Fine. I'll go."

Was ever an offer of a date accepted so grudgingly? Lucas didn't seem to mind, though, but only smiled and said, "Great. It starts at five, so I should pick you up around four-thirty—"

"No," she said, and his eyebrows went up again. "I mean," she went on hurriedly, "it's silly for you to drive all the way out to here to get me. I'll meet you in Sedona. Just let me know where."

He hesitated, then said smoothly, "Well, if we're starting in uptown, then you could park in the structure at Sinagua Plaza and meet me out front there."

Thank the Goddess he wasn't going to press the issue. At least if she had her own car there, she could make a quick getaway if necessary. And if any other McAllisters showed up, well, she could think of some way to spin it—after all, there wasn't anything so strange about one of her clan's elders going to support their prima's consort at his art exhibit, even in the company of Lucas Wilcox. He did seem to act as a sort of informal clan elder himself, and so the whole outing could be seen as two peers working together for the good of both their clans. Perfectly logical.

Unfortunately, she had a feeling neither of her fellow McAllister elders would view the situation in quite the same way, were they to discover her plans.

CHAPTER FOUR

MARGOT AGREEING TO GO OUT WITH HIM ON THE GAL-LERY walk was miracle enough. The even bigger miracle was that she hadn't called sometime during the intervening week to cancel the whole thing. He'd been expecting the call the whole time, actually—*oh, sorry, Lucas, something came up. I hope you understand*—and had mentally rehearsed his replies so his disappointment wouldn't be too blatantly obvious. Even worse would have been a text, since that would have made it clear that she didn't want to talk to him at all, not even long enough to shoot him down one last time.

But she hadn't called, or texted, and now he stood here in their designated meeting place, on the steps of the plaza as people streamed around him, talking and laughing, all intent on their various destinations. The sun had already disappeared behind the buildings on the west side of the street, and the air was cool. Well, probably downright cold to the people who lived here in Sedona or came from farther south, in Phoenix and Tucson, but to him it just felt pleasant, refreshing. Maybe as the evening wore on, he'd button up his black wool overcoat, but in the meantime he'd left it hanging open.

And there she was, moving through the crowds, a shawl in warm autumn hues thrown over her long dark dress. She'd pulled her hair back, and he felt a little twinge of disappointment. Her hair was so lovely when she let it flow loose over her shoulders.

Even so, she looked so strikingly beautiful to him that he wondered why everyone around her didn't pause to stare, to drink in this woman who looked like something not quite mortal, like a goddess come down to earth to survey her domain.

Her first words weren't exactly goddess-like, however. "Sorry I'm late," she said, sounding annoyed. "The parking structure was full, so I had to find a place farther up the street."

"It's fine," he replied at once, using his friendliest, most soothing tones. "I just got here myself."

"And you found parking?"

"Not exactly," he admitted. "I paid the valet at the resort down the hill from the structure to park my car for me."

"Resourceful." Now she sounded almost rueful, as if she wished she'd thought of that herself.

Knowing he should get things moving forward, Lucas said, "I figured we'd go to Connor's gallery first, and then decide from there which way we want to head. He told me he wasn't planning on staying too late—Angela was feeling tired and stayed home."

"By herself?" Margot asked, sounding almost alarmed...for her.

That hint of worry in her voice told Lucas she wasn't quite as detached as she wanted people to believe. "No," he told her. "Mason's with her. Angela's fine—she isn't due for another five weeks, after all."

"I'm aware of that. But twins have a tendency to come early, you know."

Actually, he didn't know, and was sort of surprised Margot possessed that bit of arcane knowledge. He wished Angela and Connor had volunteered that information, but then, they'd been acting fairly relaxed about the whole thing. Of course Angela was being careful and not doing anything to stress herself or the babies, but she also didn't seem too worried about the impending delivery. Maybe it was just that she and Connor had already been through so much together that giving birth to twins didn't seem like too big a deal to her.

"Well," he said easily, "as I told you, she has Mason with her, and Dr. Ruiz on speed dial. But Connor still wants to get back as quickly as he can."

Then Lucas offered his arm to Margot, and she paused before taking it with just the slightest tightening of her mouth, as if she wished she could have thought of some rational reason to refuse the gesture. But since she didn't, he allowed himself to enjoy the gentle pressure of her arm against his, and to breathe in her scent, subtle and sweet. Something floral, although he couldn't identify it. And was that a hint of vanilla?

Probably not a good idea to ask. He'd just let himself savor their brief closeness, even though he knew it would be over as soon as they entered the gallery. And, sure enough, once they crossed the threshold, she pulled away, pretending to be occupied with drawing off her shawl and draping it over one arm.

Oh, well. It was still something that she'd taken his arm at all. There wasn't much time to be disappointed, because Connor seemed to spot them in that instant, coming toward them with an expression on his face that managed to be both pleased and puzzled—probably because although Lucas had said he would be here, he hadn't said anything about bringing Margot, not when he wasn't sure that she wouldn't back out at the last minute.

"Thanks for stopping by," Connor said, giving a lift of his own eyebrow in Lucas' direction. That eyebrow seemed to indicate there would be questions later, but for now he seemed willing to let the matter go. "My pieces are over in this side room, but really, you should look around the whole place. Eli's brought on a bunch of new artists, so there's a lot to look at."

"Will do," Lucas said, and Margot added,

"It's impressive you were able to get this many new pieces ready, what with everything that's been going on in your life lately."

Connor hesitated, as if attempting to determine whether her remark contained some sort of jab. He appeared to let it go, however, nodding before he said with a grin, "Well, I'm enjoying my new studio space a lot…especially since Angela's been binge-watching *A Baby Story* lately. I needed something to do while I was in hiding."

Poor kid…Connor, that is. Lucas had only vaguely heard of *A Baby Story*, but it sounded like something he wouldn't want to watch a single episode of, let alone a string of them.

Even Margot looked as if she wanted to smile. But since she apparently didn't want to go on record as criticizing her *prima*, she only said, "Well, I'm sure she appreciates having the time to rest."

"Oh, yeah. She's been doing a lot of *resting* lately."

Lucas chuckled. "She might as well do it now, because in a month or so, rest is going to be the last thing on her mind."

Connor didn't appear at all daunted by the prospect of a couple of babies invading his life in the near future. "True. Anyway, you two take a look around—I can see Eli over there, signaling me."

He flashed them another grin before heading farther into the interior of the gallery. Lucas pointed toward the small room where Connor's paintings hung. "Shall we?"

Connor really did have talent. Margot had known that on an intellectual level, but the last time she'd been in this gallery, the tension had been so thick she worried that some sort of magical battle would break out between the McAllister and Wilcox contingents, and that would have been a terrible mess to clean up. Public displays of power were always so difficult to sweep under the rug, and you couldn't get much more public than a gallery in the heart of Sedona's uptown district.

This evening, though, couldn't have been more different. She hadn't spotted anyone from either clan yet, apart from Connor himself, but it was enough that she and Lucas were here together, wandering from painting to painting and chatting quite amiably about the merits of each. There were several she would have liked to purchase, actually, especially one of a stand of blazing yellow aspen trees next to a dark forest stream. It felt odd to be buying Connor's work, though, especially with him right here in the gallery, and so she let it go for now. She could always check back in a few days and see if the painting was still available.

"Do you have many of his pieces?" she asked, after they'd exhausted his collection and went on to a display from another artist, one who worked in mixed media, with gold and copper leaf highlighting the heavily applied oils.

Lucas nodded. "A few. It was hard getting him to allow me to actually buy them—he just wanted to give them to me. I told him I wouldn't take them unless he let me pay him a fair market price for them. But I knew he'd be going places if he kept up with his painting, even though at the time all he was doing was painting them and then stacking them up in his apartment and studio."

"Why would he do that?" Such behavior was mystifying to her. Surely if you were lucky enough to be gifted with such talent, it was your obligation to share it with the world, not hide it away.

For a second or two Lucas didn't say anything, but she could see his jaw tense. Then he said, sounding almost curt for him, "Damon."

That didn't really clear things up, but something in his expression told her she shouldn't push it. That same reticence kept her from making an acid comment that it was all the better, then, that Damon was gone. She had a feeling that sort of remark wouldn't go over very well at the moment.

They moved on to wander through the gallery, lingering at the pieces that captured their attention, moving more quickly past the ones that did not. Margot didn't want to acknowledge the way she and Lucas seemed to be drawn to the same sort of work—neither of them had much use for abstract art, apparently, and they both tended to appreciate most the *plein air*–style landscapes, particularly the ones that brought out the wild and powerful beauty of the high desert country.

Since Connor was busy talking to an older couple, possibly some buyers, all Lucas did was wave in his cousin's direction as they left the gallery. The next stop was a few doors down, and this time he seemed to remember that they hadn't helped themselves to any of the wine and hors d'oeuvres set out at Red Rock Illuminations.

"Sorry about that," Lucas said, handing Margot a plastic cup of white wine. "I guess I got distracted."

"It's fine," she replied, and really, it was. She'd forgotten, too, although now she found herself a bit thirsty, and so was grateful for the wine. "If we drank at every gallery, we'd be a mess by the end of the evening."

"True," he agreed, and chuckled. His expression sobered then. "I thought after this we could hit the galleries at Tlaquepaque. And—" He broke off, looking almost embarrassed.

"And?"

"Well, I hope you don't mind, but since we were going to be ending up there around dinnertime anyway, I went ahead and made us reservations at René."

So much for this not really being a date. Margot had never eaten there, but she had heard René was one of Sedona's more high-end restaurants, the sort of place that mere mortals generally reserved for birthdays and anniversaries and other special occasions. And now Lucas wanted to take her there for dinner? Not that the cost would matter to him, but surely he knew it was not the sort of place you went with a woman if you were on a casual outing.

He was watching her with those dark eyes of his, though, looking almost but not quite nervous. Waiting for her to protest, to say she didn't think the venue was at all appropriate?

Well, if that was what he expected, then she'd do the exact opposite. "That sounds wonderful," she said calmly. "I've never been, but I've heard it's very good."

At those words, he did relax visibly. "It's excellent," he assured her. "Our reservations are for seven, so we might as well take the trolley down there so we can make the rounds of the galleries before dinner."

Which was what they did, squeezing onto the open-air vehicle with a mass of tourists, and locals just wanting to get out and about. During the ride from uptown to the shopping center, Margot was all too aware of Lucas' presence behind her, the way she could feel his body pressed up against hers in the tight confines of the trolley. It was a relief when they stopped and got out. Maybe then the unwelcome warmth that had pooled somewhere in the pit of her stomach would dissipate, and she could rid her mind of the way they'd been crushed together, of how solid and strong he seemed.

If he'd been thrown off-kilter at all by that unexpected physical nearness, Lucas didn't show it. He only smiled and guided her toward the first gallery, a place that seemed to specialize in exquisite art glass, including some truly amazing ceiling fixtures.

She murmured her appreciation, and Lucas said, "Yes, I've been drawn to these pieces, too. In fact, I have one in my dining room. Maybe you can come see it sometime."

Her immediate reaction was to tell him that was impossible, that no way would she be going up to Flagstaff any time soon, let alone to his house, but there was such a hopeful light in his eyes that she didn't have the heart to refuse him point-blank. So she simply replied, "Maybe," and then pretended to be absorbed in inspecting a triptych depicting a stylized landscape at sunset.

Being Lucas, he didn't push, but gave the faintest of nods before following her around the gallery until they'd made the complete circuit. From there they went to several more, where they weren't inclined to linger, as the pieces there were too modern for their taste.

In front of the last stop was a sort of garden of copper and bronze wind sculptures, even now moving slightly, although the night was quite calm, with little wind. Margot wandered amongst them, looking at all the different configurations, and wondering if she could justify the expense of having one installed in her yard. It would look lovely, catching the sunlight, speeding up and slowing down as the capricious winds flowed over and around Cleopatra Hill.

"You like them?" Lucas asked.

"Yes. I've seen other wind sculptures here and there as I've driven around, but these are so much more substantial, so beautifully made." She pulled her shawl more closely about her; the air had only cooled further as they'd lingered in the last gallery. Maybe she should have brought a real coat.

"Which one's your favorite?"

What a question, one she had no intention of answering. Knowing Lucas, he'd put in a call tomorrow, buy it, and have someone over at her house installing it before she knew quite what had happened. "I couldn't really choose," she hedged. "They're all so lovely."

His mouth twitched, as if he'd guessed at the true reason for her reticence. "It is hard to pick one." Then he pushed back the sleeve of his overcoat slightly so he could look at his watch. "It's almost seven. We should probably head over to the restaurant now."

A situation fraught with its own perils, but at least they'd be inside, and warm. And, despite the cheese she'd nibbled two galleries earlier, she was hungry. She'd just have to do her best to keep the conversation as light and undate-like as possible.

Once again Lucas offered her his arm, and she took, knowing that protesting wouldn't do her any good. Anyway, the cobblestone walkways here were a little treacherous, and she was wearing heeled boots, so she might as well accept the support he was offering. Just something practical and friendly. Now if she could only keep her thoughts from dwelling on how strong he felt, or how…intoxicating…it was to have him this close to her.

Intoxicating?

Get a hold of yourself, she thought, keeping her chin up and what she hoped was a pleasant smile fixed on her features. *You're a grown woman, not some silly sixteen-year-old mooning over your high school's quarterback.* Not that she'd ever done such a thing; jocks had never been her type. She risked a quick glance over at Lucas and wondered if he'd played sports in school. He certainly had the build for it.

She doubted she'd have the courage to ask.

But then they were at the restaurant, and the maitre d' was smiling at Lucas and guiding them to a secluded table off in a corner. Had Lucas slipped the man a twenty to get such a prime spot? Probably not…most likely it was just more of the warlock's "luck" in action.

The place was elegant, but in a low-key way, with its muted blue-gray walls and subdued lighting. She waited while the maitre d' pulled out her chair, then sat down and set her purse and shawl on the empty seat next to her. Lucas took his place directly opposite her, for which she was glad. She'd always preferred having a dinner companion across the table rather than beside her, as at least that way she wouldn't get a crick in her neck while trying to hold a conversation.

After giving both of them menus and Lucas the wine list, the man told them their server would be along shortly. Margot opened her menu at once, glad of the opportunity to look at something else beside her companion's expectant expression. Yes, the place was expensive, but she wouldn't allow herself to worry about that. Lucas had chosen the restaurant, so certainly he didn't mind what he'd be paying for dinner.

"Any wine preferences?" he asked.

"Not really," she replied. "I'm afraid I'm not much of an expert. I do prefer reds, though."

"So do I," he said. His gaze seemed to linger on her mouth, and she wondered if she would've done better to have chosen a lighter shade of lipstick, rather than the warm brick color she wore. Then he returned his attention to the wine list. "Well, it's hard to go wrong with a Bordeaux...unless you're ordering fish."

She shook her head. "I don't really care for fish all that much. I was thinking of the antelope, just because I've never had it."

"It's excellent. And the Bordeaux will work well with that."

The waiter appeared then, and Lucas requested the wine, then waited while she placed her order. He went with steak, and they both asked for salad, and the waiter headed off to the kitchen, leaving them alone together.

Why she should feel so intimidated now, when they'd already spent the greater part of two hours together, Margot wasn't sure. Maybe it was simply that they were facing one another in a more formal setting. The gallery walk was one thing, but no one could call having dinner in this restaurant anything other than a date.

Even as she began casting about in her mind for something innocuous they could talk about, Lucas said, "You know, I'm really curious how you came to be an elder."

Oh, Goddess. That was the last thing she wanted to discuss. Maybe she could deflect him somehow. "What, don't you think I'm a strong enough witch to be an elder?"

"That's not it at all," he began, then stopped abruptly when the waiter approached their table with the wine. A brief interval while the cork was removed, and Lucas did the ritual tasting of the small amount the waiter poured into his glass. Custom satisfied, the man tipped a more substantial amount into both their glasses before saying their salads would be out soon and then departing.

Any hopes she'd had of Lucas abandoning the topic disappeared when he sipped some wine, and said, "It just seems a little strange to an outsider, is all. Angela mentioned once that you'd been an elder for almost ten years. What, were you still in college when they asked you?"

She allowed herself a small, if albeit bitter, smile. "Hardly. I was twenty-seven."

His eyebrows went up at that. "So you weren't really an elder in any sense of the word."

"That's not how it works, Lucas." Really, she shouldn't be discussing her clan's inner workings with a Wilcox, no matter what Angela might say about putting the past aside and working together for a better future for both families. But he kept gazing at her, clearly expecting her to answer, and she found herself saying, "It's not about age. Not really. True, most of the time an elder is asked to serve when he or she is older, in the prime of his or her power, but I'd always been very strong." She told him this simply, as it wasn't boasting. Her power was part of her, like the color of her eyes. She hadn't chosen it—perhaps the Goddess had chosen it for her, but the strength of her gift wasn't something Margot had precisely achieved on her own.

"So that's why? Just because you were the strongest witch?"

"One of them." Damn it, she'd tried so hard not to think about that time in her life, what the consequences of her elevation to elder had actually been. She picked up her wine and drank, attempting to focus on the dark, rich sweep of it over her tongue, and not the day all those years ago when Bryce and Allegra had come to her and said, *It is your time to serve.* Her voice hardened. "But since Allegra Moss and Bryce McAllister were already appointed elder, there really wasn't anyone else."

"Seems kind of rough, giving you that responsibility when you were so young." His tone was obviously sympathetic, but she didn't want to acknowledge that. Feeling sorry for herself, for what had happened, wouldn't change anything.

She shrugged. "It was what it was."

The waiter came back with their salads, so once again they fell silent until he was safely away. Funny how, despite their being from two such very different clans, they both followed the same unspoken rule, which was never to discuss witch business when a civilian was around. Then again, maybe it wasn't so odd. All the various clans had survived to this day because they'd learned how to be discreet.

Margot decided maybe it was time to go on the attack. "And what about the Wilcoxes? I find it kind of strange that you don't even have clan elders."

"No need, with the way the *primuses* always ran things." He speared a few pieces of radicchio with his fork but didn't lift them to his mouth. "We were more of a monarchy, I guess." His tone was almost amused, but Margot thought that note of amusement didn't ring entirely true.

"Even now, with Connor in charge?"

This time he did eat, and drank some water before he replied. "No, I'd say things are sort of in flux. It's pretty clear he has no intention of running things the way Damon, or his father before him, did. I guess in a way you could call Marie and Andre and me the unofficial Wilcox elders, since we're the ones he seems to go to for advice most of the time. At least, for Wilcox matters," he added quickly. "Obviously, he and Angela talk pretty much everything over, but she doesn't want to be seen as interfering in our family's business."

Wise of her, Margot thought. *I really wouldn't want to get embroiled in any of that, either.* "And you don't mind?"

"Why would I? I'm glad Connor feels he can rely on me." A lift of the shoulders, and he said, "I used to be Damon's sounding board, too."

"Indeed? I had no idea Damon Wilcox ever took anyone's advice but his own."

"Well," Lucas replied, after sipping some wine, "just because he used me as a sounding board doesn't mean he actually ever *did* anything I advised."

This was said in such a self-deprecating tone that Margot let out a reluctant laugh. In general, the mere mention of the late *primus* was enough to make her skin prickle, even now, when he was certainly no danger to anyone. But the way Lucas spoke of his late cousin told her that they'd had at least a friendly relationship, something she had a hard time wrapping her head around.

"Do you miss him?" she asked abruptly.

He paused a long time before answering. "Sometimes. That is, I can't excuse the things he did, because there *is* no excuse for them. And I can't fault for Angela doing what she had to do, because there really was no alternative. But…." The word seemed to hang in the air, even as he shook his head and ate another bite of his salad.

"But?" she prompted, then returned to her own neglected plate of field greens.

"We were friends," Lucas said simply. "I have a lot of friends, but he didn't. I think that's why he liked talking with me, even if he planned to do things his way in the end. And I'd meet him when he was done with classes sometimes, and we'd have a few beers and talk about the D-backs, and—"

Margot felt her eyes widening. Damon Wilcox, plotter and mastermind behind Angela's kidnapping, was just a regular guy who liked baseball? "I find that hard to believe."

A shrug. "Believe it, or don't. He had a whole lot of different sides, like most people. I suppose it's just that Damon didn't show many of his. But we'd known each other since we were kids. I think he appreciated that he could relax around me, that I never asked him for anything."

"I'd think it was the other way around," she remarked. "Don't tell me he never asked you for investment advice."

"Oh, he did that all the time," Lucas said easily. "Why not? Using my gift to help the clan seemed a natural enough thing. It didn't hurt anybody."

No, she supposed not. Well, maybe some people would call Lucas' supernatural inside information a way of gaming the system, but she really didn't think so. It really wasn't all that different from having Adam nudge a few storm clouds closer to Jerome so everyone's wilted vegetable gardens could get some much-needed rain in the midst of a long, hot summer.

"I'm sorry," she said softly, and Lucas sent her a surprised look.

"Sorry for what?"

"I'm sorry for your loss. Like you, I can't excuse or forgive Damon for the things he did, but still, it hurts when you lose a friend. So I am sorry for that."

Several indefinable emotions flitted across Lucas' face—surprise? confusion?—but then he gave her a considering nod. "Thanks, Margot."

They fell into a long silence after that, finishing their salads without speaking, waiting until the plates were taken away and their entrees brought. At last Lucas spoke.

"You're a surprising woman, Margot Emory."

"I am?" she said with a small laugh. "Really, I think I'm sadly predictable."

"Not so." Now his gaze was warm, and she forced herself not to shift nervously in her seat, to keep herself looking back at him as if being studied in such an admiring way was something that happened to her every day. "Don't sell yourself short."

Well, it was easy to do that when everyone else did. Then she chided herself for the self-pitying thought, which wasn't even true. The worst she could say of her clan members was that they expected her to be as she was: an elder, there when a dispute needed to be mediated, a spell shored up, a decision made when changes in the outside world necessitated some alteration of the clan's policies. And could she really fault them for that? They were only doing as they'd always done.

"I'll try not to," she said lightly, then looked away from him to the food on her plate, and made something of a show of cutting a few pieces and eating them slowly, making herself concentrate on the thick, rich taste of the antelope and not on the expression of the man watching her.

He seemed to take the hint, and ate quietly as well. Even when their conversation resumed, it was on lighter topics—whether there would be much snow this winter, what with the ongoing drought, and whether the maternity ward at Flagstaff Medical

Center was large enough to accommodate the hordes of Wilcoxes and McAllisters who were certain to descend as soon as the twins were delivered. Inwardly, Margot could only thank Lucas for letting the matter drop. Who knew a Wilcox could be so perceptive?

After dinner he called a cab, as it was past the time when the free trolley was running.

"We could walk," she protested. After all, it was barely half a mile from Tlaquepaque to the plaza in uptown where they'd met.

"No, thanks," he said easily. "Half a mile uphill, some of it with no street lamps. I'm not saying it's dangerous or anything, but it's really not a walk you want to make."

So she acquiesced, even though she was of the mind that the two of them could take on pretty much anything they met in that dark stretch between the shops on 179 and the more populated uptown area. But she did have to admit that, after a large meal and half a bottle of extremely good Bordeaux, it was probably better to have a cab take her back to her own car.

True, sitting next to Lucas in the back seat of the cab was a little too close quarters. His knee brushed hers once or twice, and she couldn't be sure whether he'd done so on purpose. Not that she'd call him to task about it, not with the cab driver sitting just a few feet away, but still....

At least the ride only took a couple of minutes. Almost before Margot knew it, they had stopped in front of Sinagua Plaza, and Lucas was leaning forward and handing the driver a twenty. Twenty dollars? For a half-mile ride?

She didn't say anything, though, and didn't protest when Lucas reached down to help her out of the cab after he'd pushed his tall frame out of the back seat and onto the sidewalk. Somehow she felt a little unsteady on her feet. Delayed reaction to the Bordeaux?

That had to be it.

"Where did you park?" Lucas asked as the cab eased its way out from the curb.

"Just up the street half a block, then down the side street." Realizing why he'd asked the question, she added quickly, "There's no need to walk me to my car. You'd just be going out of your way."

His eyebrow lifted. "You must really have a bad opinion of us Wilcoxes if you think I'm just going to let you walk down there alone in the dark."

Oh, of all the—"That's not what I meant."

"What did you mean?"

Obviously, she was not going to win this argument. "Fine. If you think I'm really in that much danger, here in Sedona, of all places, then by all means, come along."

She pulled her shawl more closely around herself and began walking. Lucas let out something that sounded suspiciously like a chuckle, but tagged along dutifully a pace behind her. Really, it was very well-lit here, what with the illumination from the shopping center and the lights in the parking lot of the hotel across the way from the spot where she'd left her car. All this fuss for nothing.

As she walked, she scrabbled in her purse for her keys. That way, she could have them in hand and be ready to flee at once, rather than stand there with Lucas watching as she tried to locate them amongst the wallet and the cosmetics bag and the packet of tissues and all the other items she had crowding her purse.

With her keys safely clutched in her fingers, she stopped a foot or so away from the rear of her Subaru and said, "I had a very nice time, Lucas. Thank you for dinner."

Even in the chancy lighting from the street lamps in the parking lot a hundred feet away, his dark eyes twinkled. "Nice?"

"Well—" she flailed. What else was she supposed to say? "Dinner was wonderful."

"'Wonderful' is better," he said. "And so is this."

Before she could do anything, could attempt to move away, he bent down and pressed his mouth against hers. Shocked, she could only stand there, her brain seemingly incapable of registering what was going on, that Lucas Wilcox was *kissing* her.

And what was she doing? Kissing him *back*.

His arms were around her, pulling her close. Dimly, she heard her keys drop with a *clink* to the asphalt, followed by the softer *thud* of her purse. And she was breathing him in, tasting the rich, sweet dregs of the wine and the flourless chocolate cake they'd ordered to finish off their meal. The air was cold against her skin, but she was warm, so warm, her entire body seeming on fire as she pressed against him, felt again the solid, imposing strength of his body.

No. This was insane. What the *hell* was she thinking?

Somehow she found the strength of will to put her hands up against his chest, push herself away, stumble backward until she bumped into the rear of her car. "No," she gasped. "I can't—I *won't*—do this."

His breathing sounded hoarse, uneven, and he stared down at her in consternation. "Margot—"

"No," she said again. "I can't. I'm—thank you again for dinner, Lucas."

And she bent and grabbed her purse, then her keys, and scuttled away from him, keeping the reassuring bulk of her Forester at her back, as if by doing so she could prevent Lucas from attempting to pull her into his arms again.

He didn't, though. He only stood there, watching her with sad eyes as she got into the car and gunned the engine, then drove off.

She didn't dare look back.

CHAPTER FIVE

ALL RIGHT, MAYBE HE SHOULDN'T HAVE PUSHED IT QUITE that hard. But he'd looked down into her face, seen the way she gazed at him, her lips slightly parted. In every other woman he'd ever been with, that sort of expression was a clear invitation to intimacy.

The problem was, Margot wasn't like any other woman he'd been with.

He drove home, going too fast, knowing that if he were anyone else, going fifteen miles an hour over the speed limit at nine o'clock at night on twisty 89A as it wove through Oak Creek Canyon would be an open invitation for a speeding ticket. Especially in a bright red Porsche.

But he'd never gotten a speeding ticket in his life. Or a parking ticket. Never been audited by the IRS, never broken a bone or chipped a tooth or even gotten a bad meal. Of course not. Those things happened to other people, not "lucky" Lucas Wilcox.

He hadn't been so lucky tonight, though, had he?

Even though it was probably in the forties outside, he pushed the button to pop the top, hoping the cold air rushing through his hair and over his face might help to clear his head. Instead, the contrast only seemed to intensify the memory of how warm Margot's lips had been against his, how soft and eager.

Well, eager for a few seconds, until she realized what she was doing and who she was doing it with.

"Shit," he said aloud. He'd really blown this one.

Okay, acknowledging that…how did he fix it?

Good question. It was as if she were fighting with herself, some part of her attracted to him, but the other part—the responsible part—telling her all the reasons why this whole thing could never, ever work.

And that mystified him. Okay, the McAllister/Wilcox truce was still a little new and fragile, but it was getting less new with every day that passed, and clearly there were some, like Adam and Mason, who were just fine with that. But Margot was not fine with that at all.

Somehow he'd have to figure out a way to get her to change her mind. If it were simply that she wasn't attracted to him, he'd let the whole thing go.

That wasn't it, though. He'd felt the heat between them, felt the way she pressed herself against him, opened her mouth to his. She'd wanted it...until she didn't. Why?

He didn't have the answer to that, but the next day he was going to talk to someone who might.

Normally, he would call before dropping by Connor's and Angela's house. Today, though, he hadn't wanted to get into any of this on the phone. If they were out, well, he'd try again later. It did sound as if Angela wasn't getting out much these days, except to go to the doctor's and the store, so Lucas thought he had a fairly good chance of catching her at home.

And, sure enough, she was the one to answer the door. Her eyes widened as she looked up at him, one hand pressed to the small of her back, as if standing up even this much pained her. "Lucas?"

"Hi, Angela," he replied, already feeling guilty for barging in on her so unexpectedly. All this mess with Margot must have screwed up his head even more than he thought. "Sorry I didn't call, but—"

"It's okay," she said. "Come on in. Connor didn't tell me you were coming over."

"That's because I didn't tell him."

She sent him a searching glance, as if trying to determine just by looking at him what his reason for being here really was. "Well, he's up in his studio. I can call him."

"That all right," Lucas said quickly. "I actually came over to talk to you."

For a second, she didn't reply. Then he saw her shrug. "Is this about Margot?"

"Uh—why would you ask that?"

"Because when Connor came home last night, he told me you'd been on the gallery walk with her. He said he nearly fell over when he saw you walk into Red Rock Illuminations together."

Oh, right. Of course Connor would have told Angela all about that. "Well, yes," he admitted. "I hope you don't mind me picking your brain."

"There's not much to pick, but come on in." She led him from the entry into the family room, where the flat-screen TV was paused in the middle of a scene showing a very pregnant woman. *A Baby Story?* Probably. Angela picked up the remote and turned off the TV, then settled herself with a sigh on the couch. "I'd offer you some coffee or something, but right now I'm at the stage where it's serve yourself."

"No, I'm okay," Lucas said hurriedly. The poor kid looked totally wrung out, and who could blame her? She was so big with the twins now that she appeared as if a stray breeze would topple her right over. The last thing he wanted was to make her get him something to drink.

She let out a relieved sigh, pushing a stray strand of hair away from her face. There were circles under her eyes, and she didn't seem quite as blooming as the last time he'd seen her.

"Everything okay?" he asked.

Her focus returned to him, and she smiled slightly. "I'm fine. Sleep's a little tough these days… and I'm someone who's used to sleeping on her back. No, it's just that Dr. Ruiz thinks I'm going to need a C-section, and I really didn't want to have to do that."

Lucas didn't have a lot of experience with those sorts of things, but he knew enough to ask, "Have you thought about consulting Eleanor?" The Wilcox healer had delivered a lot of babies, and he still wasn't entirely sure why Connor and Angela had decided to use a regular ob-gyn instead of the clan's healer.

"Oh, yeah, I called her first thing. She agrees with Dr. Ruiz, says she probably would've sent me to an obstetrician anyway. She did say she'd help me with the scars, that you'd never be able to tell I had surgery." Another smile, this one rueful. "As if I really care about that. It's not like I'm much of a bikini girl. But, bottom line is that these babies are big, and I'm not, and so I just have to deal with it." Angela shifted on the couch, picked up one of the throw pillows, and shoved it behind her, as if attempting to get more support for her back than the couch's regular cushions allowed. "Anyway, I'm fine. So what did you want to ask about Margot?"

In that moment he was ashamed of his intrusion, wishing he'd had the sense to stay at home and stew on the matter himself, rather than burdening Angela with it. She had enough on her plate already. But, since he was here now, he decided he might as well plunge ahead. "Well—I guess if there's anything you can tell me that'll help me figure out what's going on in her head. I'm getting some mixed signals, and I'm not sure what I should do next."

For a few seconds, Angela didn't say anything. When she did speak, her tone was gentle. "Lucas, it's your life, and you can tell me to butt out, but did you go out and choose the worst woman for you on purpose?"

"Why would you say that?"

"Because she's an elder. Because she's spent her whole life thinking of you Wilcoxes as the enemy. You don't just turn that off overnight."

That's for damn sure. But he thought again of how she had responded at first last night. He could tell she'd wanted him, if only for a few seconds before the logic centers in her brain switched on. "I get that. But…." He let the words trail off, then shrugged. "I guess I'm not willing to give up yet. So anything you can tell me would help."

"There's not much to tell." Angela reached back and tugged at the pillow in the small of her back, apparently moving it into a better position. "That is, Margot's a really private person. She lived with her mother until a about a year ago, when Sylvia moved down to Clarkdale. And Margot's illusions are amazing—I mean, I can see why they chose her to be an elder."

"About that," Lucas broke in. "She seems way too young to be an elder. How did that even happen?"

Angela replied with a lift of her own shoulders. "I really don't know. I mean, I was just in middle school when Rory McAllister died and they had to get a new elder. My Aunt Rachel told me they chose Margot, and I was just sort of, 'okay.' The thought of Margot's age didn't really occur to me, because when you're twelve, everyone seems a lot older, you know?"

He supposed he did know, or at least vaguely remembered. "But you don't recall anything else about it?"

"Not really. I was more worried about my algebra homework, frankly. Sorry, Lucas, but you'd really do better to ask Rachel about all this."

That prospect didn't sound too appealing. Yes, Rachel was beginning to loosen up a bit, mostly because she really did like Connor—pretty much *everyone* liked Connor, actually—but that still didn't mean Lucas wanted to drive down to Jerome and grill her on the subject of Margot Emory.

Angela must have noted his distinct lack of enthusiasm, because she said, "If I had anything more to tell you, I would. And really, I'm the last person to get all judge-y about impossible relationships. I think you'd be good for Margot. Whether you can convince her of that?" She let out a tiny sigh, hardly more than a breath. "I don't know."

Neither did he. Even so, Angela's remark that he'd be good for Margot buoyed him a bit. He had to keep trying. Sure, a smarter man might have decided it wasn't worth the trouble, but Lucas knew better. Last night he'd gotten just a glimpse of who she could be, if she only would allow herself, and he wasn't going to stop now.

"Thanks, Angela," he said, smiling at her, hoping she could see from his expression that he'd found her input helpful. "I know what I need to do next."

Margot lay in bed past her usual rising time of six-thirty, staring up at the ceiling, wondering if and when she finally got herself dressed and went out, whether the members of her clan would see the stain of Lucas Wilcox's kiss on her mouth like some latter-day scarlet letter. Surely it had to be visible; she swore she could still feel the pressure of his lips on hers, even twelve hours later.

No, that was silly. She knew what she had done, but since the McAllister clan didn't currently number any mind readers within its ranks, her secret should be safe enough. Apart from Connor, no one from either family had even been at the gallery walk the night before, so she hadn't been seen with Lucas. It was going to be fine.

But was it, really?

She showered and dressed, applied her makeup with care, dried her hair and ran a brush through it. The heavy locks lay loose and gleaming on her shoulders, and she decided not to pull them back today. No real reason, except that it promised to be cold, and her hair was warm against her neck. As she did each day, she scrutinized it, wondering when the first strands of gray would appear, and whether she'd wear them proudly or would cast just the tee-niest, tiniest illusion spell to cover them up.

Or do what everyone else did, and go to the drugstore for some dye to hide the evidence that she wasn't twenty-five anymore.

No white hairs had appeared overnight, despite the way she'd tossed and turned, and so she left the bathroom and went to the kitchen. The ritual of making tea calmed her a bit, and by the time she'd sat down at the small round table by the window with her Darjeeling and her sourdough toast, she could almost convince herself that this was just an ordinary day like any other.

Except it wasn't. It was the day after the night when she'd kissed Lucas Wilcox, had felt her whole body come alive in a way it hadn't for a very long time. Trying to ignore the effect he'd had on her was like telling the green grass not to grow after a much-needed rain.

And that was it. As much as she wanted to deny what he'd done to her, she couldn't. Even now, as she sipped her tea and tried very hard not to think of anything at all, memories of him kept crowding her mind—the dark eyes with their heavy fringe of lashes, the mouth that managed to be sensual and amused at the same time, the way the laugh lines around his eyes crinkled when he smiled. And the harder she tried to banish those images, the more they seemed to be the only thing she could think about.

"Damn it," she muttered under her breath, even as she rose from the table to wash out her mug and clean the crumbs off the plate. The house had a dish-washer, but she hardly ever used it. Wasteful, when it was only her living here.

Only her. In that moment, she realized how much she hated the very idea of being alone in this house. No one to talk to, no one to care what she did or didn't do. She kept it clean because it wasn't in her nature to do otherwise, but really, when you came right down to it, she could let the place go completely, and no one would even notice. Well, except her mother, maybe; Sylvia hadn't been the world's greatest housekeeper, and it was Margot who'd taken on that responsibility from about the time she was fourteen. But she'd still make a comment when she dropped by, if it turned out the place wasn't being kept up to Margot's usual high standards.

If you hate it, then get out, she told herself. *It's time to make the rounds anyway.*

So she fetched a jacket, fluffed her hair over it, and went out. She didn't bother to lock the door. No one would disturb her cottage, and besides, there wasn't anything in it she really cared all that much about.

Only now did she realize how much that thought bothered her.

Rachel McAllister had sounded mystified by Lucas' request to speak with her, but she didn't say no. She did tell him that Saturdays were busy and that she wouldn't be able to see him until after six-thirty. He'd said that was fine, even though he chafed at the delay. To take the edge off, he'd called a few friends for an impromptu round of golf, to which they'd all been agreeable. Might as well; winter was on its way, and opportunities to hit the green would be pretty scarce in the near future.

Since they were all casual acquaintances, fine for discussing the merits of a new driver or the Cardinals' prospects in the upcoming season and not much else, none of them seemed to notice his preoccupation, how he really wasn't all that focused on the game. Not that it mattered, as he still came out on top, at two under par. Normally he'd force himself to blow a few shots, just so he wouldn't always win, but today he wasn't paying the proper attention.

"Drinks?" Dave asked, dropping his putter into the bag on the back of his cart.

"Not today," Lucas replied. "I need to be somewhere at six-thirty."

A knowing grin. "Hot date?"

Well, at least Dave had relaxed a lot, now that his divorce was final. Of course, getting paid cash up front for the house that Connor and Angela now owned probably had something to do with his improved outlook on life.

"Not really."

"Hmm," was all Dave said, but Lucas could tell he wasn't quite buying it. His friends were too used to the apparently unending string of women he dated. Not that he'd added to that string in a long time. Ever since meeting Margot, his heart hadn't really been in it.

He went home and took a quick shower, then put on some jeans and a T-shirt, pulling a sweater over that. For a second he wondered if he was being too casual, then reminded himself he was going to Jerome. If anything, he probably looked overdressed.

Spatters of rain began to fall as he drove south on I-17, so he was glad he'd decided against going down through the canyon. Not that the Porsche couldn't handle it, but in his current abstracted state, he preferred the straight-line driving on the highway.

By the time he pulled up in front of the shop Rachel McAllister owned, the rain had begun to fall in earnest. Since the weather had looked iffy in the rain department, he'd worn his leather jacket instead of his wool overcoat, but the shop looked very closed. Rachel hadn't given him any specific instructions, and he waited in the car for a minute, wondering if he should pull around to the back, where he knew the private entrance to the apartment over the store was located.

But then he saw the shop door open, and Rachel herself standing there, giving him a beckoning gesture. He got out of the car and ducked his head, walking quickly to the entrance. She stepped out of the way so he could move past her, then shut the door behind him.

"Lovely weather we're having," she quipped, and he grinned at her.

"I like it."

She made a noncommittal "hmm" noise, then said, "Come on up to the apartment. If we stand by the front door, someone's going to think the store's open, and I don't feel like shooing away tourists right now. The crew I had to get rid of at six was bad enough."

"No problem," he replied, letting her take the lead and guide him up the narrow staircase to the apartment that occupied the top two floors of the building. It took some effort for him to avoid seeming too obvious as he studied his surroundings. Angela had told him about this place, but he'd never been here before. It felt cramped to him, although he wasn't sure whether that was because the place really didn't have much square footage, or because Rachel seemed to have crammed it full of antiques and knickknacks and potted plants, most surfaces taken up by framed pictures of family members or crystals or figurines carved from stone.

Above all that, though, he smelled something rich and spicy emanating from the kitchen. He must have lifted an eyebrow, because Rachel said, "I've had beef barbacoa going in the crock pot all day. Of course you'll be staying for dinner."

"Oh, no—I didn't expect you to feed me—"

"Maybe you didn't, but I'm still going to." Her hazel eyes twinkled. "But I have some last-minute things to do, so I hope you don't mind chatting in the kitchen."

He knew better than to protest. Besides, Rachel's cooking was supposed to be spectacular. She'd taught Angela, after all, and the girl was definitely no slouch in that department herself.

Rachel washed her hands, and then pulled an onion and a pepper from the ancient refrigerator. After setting down a scarred butcher-block cutting board, she set to work, chopping the vegetables with a brisk, easy efficiency that put the chefs on those cable cooking shows to shame. "I suppose you want to talk to me about Margot."

"I—" What the hell? He hadn't said anything about why he wanted to see Rachel, only that he hoped she had time for a quick chat.

A corner of her mouth twitched as she attempted to repress a smile. "Angela called me to give me some warning." The knife glinted in the light from the aged brass fixture overhead as she continued to chop away. "And I feel like I should be giving you some warning, too. Are you trying to make your life complicated?"

He hoped he hadn't driven all the way down here just to get a lecture. "Look, I know you're still not thrilled about the whole McAllister/Wilcox situation, but—"

"That doesn't have anything to do with it," she said, interrupting him, but so gently that he couldn't really take offense. "Well, actually, it does, but not because of my feelings on the matter." Vegetables chopped, she went to a skillet already sitting on the stovetop and dropped a pat of butter into it.

"Then what is it?" he asked, hoping he didn't sound too desperate and guessing that he probably did. "I know it's not as if you expect your elders to take a vow of celibacy or something. The other two are married, right?"

"Yes," Rachel replied slowly, not looking up as she stirred rice into the melted butter, and then added the chopped vegetables and some minced garlic she had sitting off to the side. "The thing is, they were both married *before* they were made elders."

"So?"

She turned away from the stove and met his gaze directly. "I'm sure Margot would probably kill me for telling you this, but it's not that it isn't common knowledge—well, among my generation, anyway. She was engaged when she was called to be an elder, and her fiancé just didn't want to deal with the implications of that. He broke it off a month before the wedding."

The word escaped Lucas' mouth before he could stop it. "Asshole."

To his surprise, Rachel nodded. "More or less. Luckily, he was with the branch of the family over in Prescott, so it's not as if she's been tripping over him continually for the past ten years, but it still was rough on her. As far as I know, she hasn't even tried to be with anyone since."

Ten years...with no one? He had a hard time even comprehending that level of loneliness. "I still don't see why her being made an elder would be such a big deal."

"Well, you Wilcoxes don't have elders the way we do. It's sort of being a city council member, a marriage and family counselor, a real estate agent, and an attorney all rolled into one. You're basically on call all the time to handle family business. It's one thing if you're already married and settled—Bryce was in his early fifties when he got the call, and Allegra around forty-seven, if I'm remembering correctly. Their marriages were stable, their kids already out of grade school or even in high school. It was an adjustment, but they could handle it. But thinking you're going to have your wife all to yourself, only to discover that you're going to have to share her with the whole clan?" Rachel shook her head, then picked up a can opener and began to open up some tomatoes. "Clay couldn't handle it. So he backed out."

"Clay, huh?"

Once again her mouth twitched at the disapproval in his tone. "Yes, Clay McAllister. Like I said, from over in Prescott. They met at Great-Aunt Ruby's seventy-fifth birthday party, as the Prescott

McAllisters generally keep to themselves, but they did show up for that occasion. Good-looking man."

"Of course he was."

Now smiling openly, she dumped the tomatoes into the skillet. "I don't think you have too much to worry about on that front, Lucas. Anyway, you can see why Margot is gun-shy. She doesn't think anyone would be willing to take on everything that comes with having an elder as a significant other. So she hasn't even tried. And now you come along, and you think because Connor and Angela made things work, that magically every other Wilcox/McAllister pairing is going to work as well. But it's not that easy."

"I don't want easy," he told her. About a million thoughts were raging in his head, foremost among them the desire to drive to Prescott, find this Clay person, and punch him in the face. Hard. But that wouldn't solve anything, would only make matters far, far worse. "Margot needs to realize that just because Clay was a cowardly prick, it doesn't mean every man who's interested in her is."

"No, you're definitely not cowardly," Rachel agreed. "But you don't have much frame of reference, either. You see things going fine for Connor and Angela, and maybe in the back of your head you think it should be the same for Margot. The problem is, Angela was barely a *prima* before her entire world changed. She doesn't see why there should be an issue with her splitting her time between here and Flagstaff, because she hasn't spent the past ten years being available whenever the people in her clan needed her. But Margot has all that history, and it's not going to go away just because you want it to."

Put that way, the prospect of getting Margot to change her mind did seem fairly daunting. But there had to be a way. He wasn't going to give up that easily. "Okay, I understand that," he said at length. "But she has to understand that history isn't necessarily destiny."

"True," Rachel replied. "And I wish you luck in convincing her of that. In fact," she added, as Lucas heard the front door to the apartment open and muffled voices coming from the tiny entry, "you can start right now."

And as Lucas began to frown at her in confusion, he saw Rachel's "friend" Tobias and Margot come around the corner of the dining room, and realized what Rachel had been planning all along.

CHAPTER SIX

TO TELL THE TRUTH, IF SHE HADN'T BEEN SO ON EDGE after her "date" with Lucas, she probably wouldn't have accepted Rachel's invitation to dinner in the first place. But when Margot had stopped by for a brief chat during her rounds, Rachel had made the offer, and at the time it sounded infinitely better than a Saturday night home alone with a book and a bowl of soup.

Now, though, Margot paused in the cramped dining room just outside the kitchen and wanted to flee. Because there was Lucas, leaning casually against the counter as if he'd done so a thousand times, watching as Rachel made Mexican rice. His gaze slid over to Margot, and she realized that, even though his posture looked relaxed, he was anything but. He hadn't been expecting this, either.

"Hello, Lucas," she managed to say, and the slow smile she'd already come to recognize spread across his lips.

"Hi, Margot," he returned. "Guess you couldn't resist Rachel's barbacoa, either."

Just the right note, friendly and unconcerned, as if the two of them meeting like this was something that happened every day. Margot could feel Tobias' gaze on her and wondered how much he really knew. It seemed clear enough that Rachel had some idea of what was going on between Lucas and herself, with information probably supplied by Angela. Whether Rachel had said anything to Tobias, Margot wasn't sure. Then again, Lucas might have mastered the art of appearing as if he didn't have a care in the world, no matter what might be going on around him, but she wasn't sure she was quite that skilled. She could have given something away, even while thinking she had everyone around her fooled.

"Do you need help with anything, Rachel?" she asked, hoping the words didn't sound too strangled.

"Not at all," Rachel replied. "The table's set, and Tobias will help me get everything transferred over. Lucas, there's a bottle of wine on the sideboard. Do you mind opening it? The corkscrew's in the middle drawer."

"Sure," he said, pushing off from the counter where he'd been leaning and coming into the dining room. Luckily, the sideboard was on the opposite side of the space from where Margot stood, so at least he didn't have to brush past her to get to it.

Tobias went on into the kitchen to assist Rachel, and so Margot found herself strangely at loose ends as she lingered in the no man's land between the dining and living rooms. She watched Lucas head toward the aforementioned bottle of wine, extract the opener from a drawer in the sideboard, and begin to extricate the cork. Since Tobias and Rachel were clattering away in the kitchen, Margot decided it was safe to speak.

"Since when do you make a habit of having dinner with Rachel McAllister?"

"I don't," he said easily, twisting at the corkscrew. "But we had a few things to talk about."

Margot had a pretty good idea what those "things" were. Casting a quick glance toward the kitchen, she replied in an undertone, "Why can't you just let it go?"

He paused then, dark eyes meeting hers in a stare that made a shiver run down her back. "Because I don't want to."

What she possibly could have said in reply, she had no idea, but Tobias came in then carrying the big pot of the barbacoa meat, and Rachel followed with a bowl of rice and a bowl of beans, and by the time the other odds and ends had been set out—tortillas, cotija cheese for crumbling, a big glass bowl of Caesar salad—the opportunity to say anything at all was lost.

Conversation wasn't as awkward as she thought it might be, either, as Rachel asked Lucas about Angela, and he said she was doing fine but was looking a little tired, as might be expected. The talk flowed about the impending arrival of the twins, and the upcoming preparations for Thanksgiving and all the holiday hubbub that would follow afterward. Lucas asked a question here and there, complimented Rachel on the food, said he hoped Margot hadn't gotten too damp on the walk over here, and in general acted like a model dinner guest. She wasn't quite that nonchalant, but she did manage to respond normally to most questions put to her, and even laughed at Lucas' jokes without sounding as if she were pretending.

Through it all, though, it was difficult to keep herself from staring at him. She wanted to gaze at the long, strong fingers as they wrapped around the stem of his wine glass, the way his heavy dark hair waved back from his brow, the fine shape of his mouth… the mouth that seemed as if it had been created to match precisely with hers. At that thought, she felt a sudden heat burn through her, and she reached for her own wine glass and took an over-large gulp, then coughed.

"Are you all right, Margot?" Rachel asked.

"Fine," Margot got out. "I must have swallowed something wrong."

Rachel appeared unconvinced, but she let it drop, instead asking Tobias if he thought the rain was going to keep up all night, or whether it would blow by quickly. Margot had to hope for the latter, as she'd already gotten somewhat damp on the walk over and was only now drying out.

"The wind was pretty brisk, so I doubt the rain will hang around long. It usually doesn't," Tobias said.

Well, that was true enough. The storms in this part of the world were intense, but in general they did what they had to do in a brief period of time before moving on. It was hard to tell exactly what was going on outside, as Rachel had the curtains drawn, and there was still the third floor of the building above their heads, effectively blocking any sound of raindrops hitting the roof.

The conversation drifted to the coming winter, and whether there would be much snow, or whether the drought would continue to limit the number of storms passing through. Before she knew it, Tobias was clearing the dinner plates and Rachel was bringing out some of her homemade flan. Where she expected her dinner guests to put it, after everything else they'd consumed, Margot wasn't sure.

She did manage to eat most of hers, just because it was too good not to, and then it was time to wrap things up, and do what she could to slide out of there gracefully before Lucas could see what she was doing. Not that her ploy worked, as he saw her struggling into her raincoat and came over to retrieve his own jacket from the coat rack.

"Can we talk outside for a minute?" he asked.

"The rain—"

"If it's raining, we can go to the Spirit Room and have a drink."

That sounded even less appetizing than standing and talking to him in the pouring rain...or at least far more dangerous...but the only way to say no was to be downright rude, and he didn't deserve that. "Okay," she said reluctantly, and buttoned up her raincoat. Her dripping umbrella was still downstairs in the short tiled corridor that led to the back entrance, so she'd have to fetch it on her way out.

They said their goodbyes to Tobias and Rachel, then went down the stairs to the ground floor. As it turned out, Margot didn't need her umbrella after all; when Lucas opened the door for her, the whole world was dark and dripping, but the rain had stopped falling. Above, a gibbous moon flickered in and out of the fast-racing clouds.

"I didn't plan that, you know," Lucas said, almost as soon as the door shut behind them.

"I know." She tightened her grip around the umbrella, not looking at him. "That was Rachel's doing. I guess she wanted to make sure we could get along like adults."

"Which we did."

"Yes." They'd been walking down toward Hull Avenue, and she realized she was unconsciously heading back toward her place. That wouldn't do at all. No way was she taking Lucas Wilcox to her house. She stopped on the corner and said, "Look, Lucas—"

"She told me."

"What?" Margot replied, taken aback by the interruption. "Told you what?"

"About Clay. About how you wouldn't give anyone a chance after that."

Fury burned through her then, which was good, because the air blowing in from the north was cold, so cold, and she needed the fire in her veins to combat it. "She had no right to tell you that."

"She said it was fairly common knowledge among your clan…at least, the people who were old enough at the time to understand what was going on." His mouth twisted, and he added, "If it makes you feel any better, she tried to warn me off."

"She didn't do a very good job of it," Margot snapped, and began walking again.

Of course he didn't take the hint, but kept striding along behind her, like a stray dog that thought it would get a good meal if it followed her home. She stopped again, this time in front of Spook Hall; no events were planned for this Saturday night, so the building was dark and empty.

"Lucas, I'm going home. I'm sorry you drove all the way down here for nothing, but—"

"It wasn't for nothing. Rachel fed me a very good meal." He stood there, staring down at her, and once again she could feel her cheeks flush, could feel a tingle move over her at the intensity of his gaze. Damn it, why was it so hard to be indifferent to him, when she'd become an expert at freezing out any man who evinced so much as a modicum of interest?

"Well, then," she said, attempting a tone of brittle carelessness. She wasn't sure how well the comment went over, though.

He didn't move, didn't blink. "Just tell me one thing. One thing, and then I'll leave you alone. Okay?"

"Okay." That sounded safe enough. She hoped. Anything to get him to back off, to let her retreat to her lonely little shell where she didn't have struggle with her body's unwelcome responses to a man who was utterly wrong for her.

"Tell me you felt nothing when I kissed you."

Oh, Goddess. One lie, and she would be rid of him. The trouble was, would he believe it?

She took in a breath, expelled it, and said, "I felt nothing."

For the longest moment, he didn't reply. Then, "You're lying."

Now was the time to protest, to say of course she wasn't lying. But that would only be piling one lie on top of another, and for some reason she couldn't bring herself to do that.

"So I'm lying. It doesn't change the fact that this is impossible, and *you're* being impossible." She turned on her heel and began walking again, not bothering to wait for his reaction. A second or two later, she heard the sound of his footsteps behind her. So he really was going to follow her all the way back to her house.

Would she have the courage to shut him out?

As they walked, the rain began to fall again, lightly at first, and then with increasing strength. Grimly, she popped open her umbrella and hastened her strides. By the time they reached her front porch, the rain was falling in sheets, and Lucas' hair was plastered to his scalp, the water sluicing off his leather jacket. Of course she couldn't leave him outside in this.

"Come on in," she said with some irritation. How like him to force her into taking him inside her home. Then again, it wasn't as if he'd brought the rain. That wasn't his talent, after all.

Unless his talent made the rain come so she'd be compelled to offer him shelter. Damn. She really had no idea how far this gift of his extended, how much it pushed and pulled on the world around him to make it form to what he wanted.

There was a coat tree in one corner of the tiny entry, so she unbuttoned her raincoat and hung it up, then watched as Lucas divested himself of his rain-slick garment and draped it from the arm of the coat tree next to hers. With one hand, he reached up and pushed his sodden hair off his forehead.

"I'll get you a towel," she said crisply, going down the hall to the linen closet. After fetching a spare hand towel, she returned to the foyer and gave the towel to him.

"Thanks." He immediately began blotting his hair, getting rid of the worst of the moisture. His shoes were dripping, too, so Margot went on,

"Take those off, and bring them into the living room. I'll get a fire started, and you can set them on the hearth to dry off."

She could only hope that by being as brisk and businesslike as possible, he'd understand that she was only doing these things because she didn't want him to be uncomfortable or catch cold, and not because she was encouraging him in any way.

How successful she was, she didn't know, but at least he was silent as he slipped off his loafers, then followed her into the living room. At this time of year, she always had logs stacked and ready to go, since the nights were chilly, and her hundred-year-old cottage had its fair share of drafts. One flick of her finger toward the hearth, and the fire blazed up at once, warm and inviting, banishing the drafts for the moment.

"So can most witches do that?" Lucas asked, towel still pressed against his head as he settled down on the couch, which wasn't much bigger than a love seat and creaked faintly under his weight.

"Can't you?"

"No," he replied, giving his hair one last blot. He looked down at the towel as if not quite certain what he should do with it, so she let out a sigh and retrieved it from him, then folded it and placed it on a corner of the hearth. "I've seen Connor do it, and Angela do it, and of course Damon could. Some of the other Wilcoxes, too, but not all. And the McAllisters?"

"Some can, some can't." She shrugged. "I'd say it depends on the strength of your primary talent, but I know yours is fairly powerful, even though it's not as obvious as some others." Since she was being forced to play hostess anyway, she asked, "Do you want some hot tea or coffee? You got pretty soaked out there."

"Coffee," he said at once, and she wasn't sure whether she should be relieved or not. It would take longer to make, which meant more time spent away from him in the kitchen, where she could try to get her roiling thoughts together. On the other hand, an offer of coffee usually meant some lingering, as her coffeepot made far more than her teapot did.

Well, not much she could do about it now. She went off to the kitchen, wondering what on earth she'd gotten herself into.

Lucas watched Margot leave the room, while at the same time trying his best not to seem as if he was watching her. She wore a pair of slim jeans tucked into high black boots and a snug-fitting black sweater, and he couldn't help but admire the view as she walked away from him.

But then she was out of sight, so he transferred his attention to the room around him. Unlike Rachel's apartment, the chamber where he sat was almost plain, each item in it clearly chosen to be in one particular place and that place only. Over the fireplace was a plein air–style painting of a stand of cottonwoods. A local artist? Probably. In the center of the mantel was an old copper bowl containing pinecones that smelled faintly of cinnamon, and to either side of that were copper candlesticks with half-burned ivory tapers sitting in them. Wooden blinds covered the windows, and a worn Persian rug in shades of brown and muted blue and rust covered the wooden floor.

There was something peaceful about the place, quietly welcoming…very unlike its owner, he thought with a quick quirk of his lips. It was all very clean and neat, too, which he liked. He could remember a few dates ending badly because he'd gone home with a woman and discovered that her house was a disaster. Maybe that shouldn't matter, but he liked order, and apparently Margot did, too. And obviously she hadn't been expecting company, which meant she kept her home like this all the time.

He heard her moving around in the kitchen and wondered if he should have offered to help. Probably not—he'd gotten the distinct impression that she was glad to get away from him to make the coffee. So he'd let her have her space…for now. Their conversation wasn't over, not by a long shot.

It did hearten him that she hadn't been able to maintain the lie, hadn't been able to deny the spark that had flared between them the previous night. At least now he understood why she was so reticent to get involved with anyone, but that didn't mean he intended to back off. One bad experience shouldn't be enough to affect your entire life. He wondered why none of the McAllister men hadn't attempted to approach her after a reasonable period had passed. Yes, she could be a damn prickly woman when she wanted to be, but she was also strong and smart and beautiful. Surely they couldn't be that cowardly.

No, that was probably too strong a word. But it seemed obvious enough that no one had wanted to make the effort. Lucas would consider that a damn shame, except that their reticence had allowed Margot to remain single all this time. He supposed he should be thanking them for leaving her alone.

She reappeared holding a silver tray laden with one of those old-fashioned cowboy-style coffeepots, a pair of sturdy brown-glazed mugs, and a little pot of milk or cream and a small bowl of sugar cubes.

"I thought you didn't drink coffee," he pointed out, even as he lifted a carved geode candle holder out of the way so she'd have room to set the tray down on the table.

"Usually, I don't." With the coffee service safely in place, she came and sat down on the couch—at a safe distance, about as far as she could get from him without actually climbing over the sofa's arm. "This was my mother's, but she got an automatic coffeemaker when she moved out. I keep it and some fresh coffee around just because Bryce likes it, and sometimes I have meetings for us elders here at the house." Her mouth tightened for a few seconds, and then she went on, "Anyway, I didn't have any cream, so I hope you're okay with milk."

"Not a problem," he said. "I take it black anyway."

Her nose wrinkled, but she just nodded and filled one of the mugs, then the other. As she busied herself adding so much milk and sugar that her coffee was probably more like coffee-flavored ice cream than the real thing, Lucas repressed a smile and took the mug clearly intended for him, wrapping his hands around it to get rid of the last of the chill from the rainy walk over here. With no milk to cool it down, the coffee wouldn't be drinkable for a while, but he didn't mind. That simply gave him more time to linger on the couch here with Margot. At the moment, he couldn't think of anyplace he'd rather be.

He couldn't say the same for her, though. Now that she was done doctoring her coffee, she perched on the edge of the couch a few feet away from him, blowing on the steaming contents of her cup in what seemed to him a desperate attempt to avoid conversation.

It's not that easy, Margot, he thought, although he blew on his own coffee a few times as well, just to be companionable. "I really didn't mean to barge in on you," he began.

"Here, or at Rachel's?"

"Both, I suppose, although that one's all on Rachel as far as I'm concerned. I just wanted to talk to her."

"Behind my back," Margot said with some bitterness.

Lucas shifted on the couch so he was almost but not quite facing her. "What else was I supposed to do? You wouldn't talk to me. Believe me, Margot, I've been with women where there just wasn't any chemistry, and I walked away. But with you? With us? There's something. You can ignore it, but that won't make it go away. And when I come across something like that, I'm not willing to let it go that easily. So yeah, I went and talked to Rachel. Maybe it was a junior high school kind of thing to do. I don't know. I just couldn't figure out what else to do."

No reply at first. Her eyes were still downcast, seeming to study the pale tan contents of her coffee mug, but he could almost hear the gears turning in her head. "You're right."

"I—what?" he said, shocked that she was agreeing with him.

"It *was* a junior high school kind of thing to do."

Damn. He knew he shouldn't have gotten his hopes up. "All right, so I have the emotional maturity of a thirteen-year-old."

Her lips quirked. "Well, I wouldn't go so far as to say that."

"What would you say?"

She took a sip of coffee, gave an almost-wince, then replied, "I'd say if your current strategy is to keep at me until you wear me down, then it might be working."

At first he wasn't sure he'd heard correctly. "It's… working?"

"Well, I'm certainly getting tired of trying to fend you off." Another sip of coffee, and she added, "I suppose I'm vaguely curious as to what you're expecting out of this pursuit you're currently engaged in. Are you just out for a quick lay, or are you looking for the house with the 2.5 kids and the dog?"

He'd known she was a no-nonsense sort of person, but for some reason he'd never thought she would state the matter quite so baldly. "If I only wanted a quick lay, I could've gotten that any time in Flagstaff without having to resort to all these extreme measures."

"Too bad."

"Excuse me?"

This time she actually smiled, then set her coffee down on a slate coaster. "That would be easier, wouldn't it? Just sex? I mean, there aren't really any logistics involved in that sort of thing. Just scratch the biological itch and get it over with."

Had he slipped into some sort of alternate reality? Was Margot proposing that they have sex and then just walk away? "I—" He cleared his throat. "I'm not so sure about the 2.5 kids, but I guess I'm leaning more toward that side of the spectrum than mindless sex, Margot."

"Well, that makes it a lot more difficult, then, doesn't it?"

"I don't think it has to."

The half-amused expression disappeared abruptly, and she glanced away, seeming to stare into the dancing flames within the hearth. After a long pause, she said, "I assume if you were picking Rachel's brain about my past, then she probably also told you something about what it means to be an elder."

"Some, yes." At last he lifted the mug to his lips and drank. The coffee was good—better than he'd expected from someone who claimed she didn't make it very often. "Do you think that's really enough to scare me off?"

"It should."

"Why? The other two McAllister elders are married, and it doesn't seem to have mattered much to them."

"Because they were already married. Their lives had already been set. There's no room for courtship for an elder, Lucas. I have to be available to my clan all the time, because I never know when something is going to come up."

"And how often has anything actually come up over the last few months?" he asked calmly. "I mean, now that you don't have to worry about the threat from us Wilcoxes."

Her mouth pursed. "All right, it's been quiet lately. But that doesn't necessarily mean anything. You can't predict when a crisis is going to occur.

That's why it's a crisis—it comes out of the blue, and then you have to drop everything and deal with it."

Undeterred, he replied, "Well, I say we put that to the test."

"How?"

"Come stay with me in Flagstaff for a few days."

Eyes flaring open, she exclaimed, "Are you crazy?"

"Not that I'm aware of."

"Sorry, Lucas, but despite what I said about casual sex a minute ago, I don't think I'm quite ready for that."

Despite the dimness of the room, he could see the blush tinging her fair skin. He fought back a chuckle. "Don't worry, Margot—I meant you could stay in the guest room."

She began to shake her head, and he went on,

"Really. Come up for a few days, see the town, and if the world doesn't end, maybe you can reevaluate your stance on this whole 'no courtship for an elder' thing."

Dead silence. He could see the tension in her jaw, the set of her mouth. It seemed clear enough to him that she hadn't expected to be challenged quite so openly. Finally she said, "And if something does go wrong—if I'm urgently needed here—you'll drop this thing once and for all?"

"Of course." Lucas didn't have much of a prob-lem making that promise, because he knew nothing was going to go wrong. Margot would come up to Flagstaff, he'd take her around, show her the local sights, wine and dine her, and after two or three days, she'd realize what she'd been missing and fall right into his arms.

Okay, it probably wasn't going to be quite that easy, but he was fairly certain that Jerome would sur-vive just fine without her for a few days.

She sat, rigid, every tense line of her body reveal-ing how conflicted she was over the whole thing. Lucas hardly dared to breathe until she spoke again.

"Fine," she said. "I'll go to Flagstaff with you."

CHAPTER SEVEN

BRYCE HAD BEEN LESS THAN THRILLED BY THE PROSPECT, but after Margot had tersely informed the other two elders that she would be out of town for two days, three at the very most, Allegra had taken her aside, smiled, and said, "You have a good time, and don't worry about us." Her blue eyes took on a sly glint as she added, "I wouldn't mind spending a few days in Flagstaff with a man who looked like that."

Margot had, of course, been mortified, and made her escape immediately afterward. Even so, she'd felt perversely pleased that at least one of her peers seemed to be on her side. And although she'd considered calling her mother directly to tell her where she was going, Margot decided that wasn't necessary. The news had probably started moving through the

McAllister grapevine almost as soon as she walked out Allegra's door.

Now Margot was driving toward Flagstaff, letting Siri guide her in, based on the address Lucas had given her. That was one thing Margot had been adamant about—she might have agreed to stay with the Wilcox warlock for a few days, but she was going to be damn sure she had her own car there in case she needed to make a hasty getaway.

For whatever reason.

It was a beautiful day at least, and she had to remind herself to keep her eyes on the road as she ranged up the interstate into territory she'd never seen before, where the freeway was lined on either side with what seemed like endless miles of ponderosa pines, flashing by so they merged into an unending sea of deep, deep green. Back in Jerome, the other trees still held onto their autumn color, but at this elevation the oaks and sycamores and cottonwoods were already bare. But they were lovely, too, their branches smooth and elegant in the slanting November sunlight.

She pulled off the highway as instructed, and began curving her way through a neighborhood of large, expensive-looking homes, most of them surrounded by their own stands of pine. The road wound around a gentle hill, moving upward until she came to a house at the end of a cul-de-sac. At that point Siri seemed to get confused, telling Margot to make U-turn, and so she switched off the navigation program. Anyway, as she approached the driveway, she spotted a mailbox with "Wilcox" engraved on a neat brass plate on the side, so she knew she was in the right place.

Lucas had told her to pull into the driveway, so that was what she did, feeling very conspicuous. All right, the place actually did appear fairly private, since it sat on a large lot, and pine trees surrounded it on three sides. Even so, she couldn't help thinking the neighbors would see her car sitting in front of the garage for days on end and would draw their own conclusions as to exactly why she was spending time with Lucas Wilcox.

Even as she began to turn off the engine, however, the door on the far right garage bay—there were three—began to open, and Lucas stepped out. She pushed the button to roll down the window and gave him an inquisitive look.

"I thought you might feel better if you could park inside."

She did, immeasurably, but she only gave him a brief nod. "Thank you, Lucas."

He wore a faint smile, as if he'd guessed precisely what she'd been thinking. "No worries." Then he stepped out of the way so she could pull into the garage. In the bay next to her was a bright red Porsche, and beyond that the dark bulk of what she thought was some kind of SUV, although she couldn't see what type.

Knowing Lucas, I doubt it's a Ford, she thought ruefully, turning off the engine and pulling her keys from the ignition.

He'd followed her into the garage, and stood waiting as she climbed out of the driver's seat. "Pop the trunk, and I'll get your luggage."

Such as it was. "You don't have to—"

"I refuse to make a lady carry her own suitcases."

This was said with such a disarming smile that Margot could only lift her shoulders in response. "Have it your way. There are only two anyway."

"That does make it easier." He pulled both her suitcases out of the trunk, one an airline-regulation wheeled case, although Margot had never been on an airplane in her life, and the other a small black leather satchel her mother had given her a few years back. Why precisely Sylvia had thought that an appropriate gift, when Margot never went anywhere, she wasn't sure, but at least it was coming in handy now.

Lucas picked up both pieces with ease, saying over his shoulder, "Right this way."

They walked around the other two vehicles, then through a door that opened into the kitchen. Margot tried to keep her eyes from widening, as that kitchen was bigger than her living room. "Cook much?" she inquired, looking at the apparent acres of granite countertop and the professional-grade stainless-steel appliances.

"Not at all," Lucas said cheerfully.

Rachel would probably spit bullets if she heard that. Her tiny kitchen was even smaller than the admittedly cramped one in Margot's own cottage. Then again, Rachel managed to create works of art in that postage stamp of a kitchen, whereas it didn't sound as if Lucas even boiled water in his, again proving the old saying that it wasn't what you had, it was what you did with it.

But that thought led Margot's mind to exactly what that old saying had actually been referencing, and she felt the heat rise in her cheeks as she followed Lucas past the dining room and up the stairs, all the while trying not look around and stare. She'd known his house would be impressive, but she hadn't known it would be quite this stunning. Twenty-foot ceilings with tongue-and-groove covering them, a massive stone fireplace that reached to the ceiling, enormous windows, every one of them filled with views of ponderosa pines.

It reminded her of something she'd read in a book once, of an inner-city student in New York wistfully writing of living someplace where she could have "windows with trees in them." Well, this place definitely had windows with trees in them....

"Here we go," Lucas said, leading her into a room twice the size of her own bedroom at home, with sturdy Craftsman-style furniture in dark oak, and a comforter with a subtle Southwest pattern of rust and blue and gold on the bed. He set her bags down on the floor next to the dresser. "That's empty, so if you want to put anything away—"

"That's fine," she said hastily. Yes, she'd do some unpacking later, but not with him watching her.

"This room has its own bathroom," he went on, hardly noting the interruption. "Right through there." And he pointed to an opening just past the closet. "Nice and private."

She definitely saw the glint in his dark eyes when he said "private." Teasing her, probably, for jumping to conclusions a few days ago and thinking he expected her to share his own room. Well, she wasn't about to acknowledge the hint. Anyway, it did feel good to know that this bedroom had its own *en suite* bath, and so she wouldn't have to be wandering the hallways of his house in her robe and slippers.

"It's lovely," she said honestly.

"Well, I'll let you settle in. Just meet me down in the family room when you're ready."

So polite, so casual and friendly, as if she were an old friend—a platonic one at that—instead of a woman he'd made no secret of his interest in. But although she couldn't claim to know Lucas well, she did know that was just his way. At any rate, she was glad of having a little private time to catch her breath and regroup before being with him.

"Thanks, Lucas. I'll just be a couple of minutes."

He nodded and went out, and she resisted the impulse to close the door. No, she'd only get the more fragile pieces out of her suitcase so they wouldn't wrinkle too badly, and put her toiletries in the bathroom, then run a brush through her hair and refresh her lipstick. The rest of it could wait for later; she didn't want Lucas to think she was hiding in here, delaying the moment when their three days together would really begin.

Never mind that that was exactly what she wanted to do.

She hung up the dresses and jacket she was concerned about, and dug her cosmetic bag and a few other items out of the suitcase and went into the bathroom. It was just as lovely as the rest of the house, with custom Mexican tile and dark cabinets and warm slate on the floor. The fixtures were dark rubbed bronze, and fluffy terra-cotta-colored towels waited for her on no fewer than three separate racks.

Trying to impress me, Lucas? she thought. If that was his intent, he was doing a fairly good job of it. Yes, she'd known that the Wilcoxes did pretty well for themselves, and Lucas more than most, but this house just seemed to point out all the shortcomings in her own cottage, which, face it, had been due for an overhaul for some years, as its last remodel had been done sometime in the '50s…and her bathroom had the pink tile to show for it. Every time she went in there, she wanted to wrinkle her nose.

But she wouldn't allow herself to dwell on that, instead pulled out her brush and gave her hair a quick once-over, then dabbed on some more lipstick. She really hadn't known what to expect from this outing, so she was wearing jeans and a dark wine-colored sweater and brown ankle boots. One of the pieces Angela had made a while back, an amethyst crystal point topped with a faceted amethyst and traced with delicate silver wire, snuggled in the hollow of her throat. The ensemble should be fine for most outings, she guessed, and if Lucas planned to take her to a five-star restaurant or something, well, then, she'd just have to come back and change.

As she descended the staircase, she heard the faint murmur of a television from somewhere toward the back of the house, so she headed in that direction. Sure enough, there was Lucas in what had to be the family room, a clubby "man cave" kind of place, with its walls painted dark green and dark brown leather sofas. An enormous flat-screen TV hung on one wall, embedded in a cabinet above another fireplace. At the moment, the screen was displaying some kind of golf tournament. When Margot entered the room, he picked up the remote and turned off the television.

"Just catching up," he said, sounding almost apologetic.

"Angela mentioned that you played," Margot replied. "Is it an important match?"

"Not really." He stood up, his manner almost diffident, as if, now that he actually had her here, he wasn't quite sure what to do with her. After a pause, he shoved his hands in the pockets of his jeans and said, "I thought maybe we'd go downtown. You can see Connor's gallery, some of the local sights. That sound good?"

"It sounds fine," she told him. Actually, she was interested to see the place where Angela had stayed for most of the winter, even though she knew it was now occupied by Connor's cousin Mason. And going around downtown would give her some much-needed points of reference.

He seemed relieved that she hadn't offered any protest. "Great. Did you bring a jacket? It's probably a good deal chillier here than what you're used to."

Oh. She should have thought of that. "I did, but it's still in the back seat of my car."

"That's fine. We'll get it when we go out to the garage."

She was already holding her purse, so there wasn't much else to do except follow him through the house, then make a brief detour to get her coat. To her surprise, he led her over to the SUV—which turned out to be a BMW—rather than the Porsche. She raised an eyebrow, and he said,

"I figured this might be a little more your speed. Not quite so flashy."

Well, she wasn't really sure a BMW was much more her speed than a Porsche, but at least it was black and not a sports car. She climbed into the passenger seat, and waited as he came around to the driver's side and got in. Being in the car with him like that, having him so close to her…it seemed a little overwhelming. Something about him felt so much larger in close quarters.

She took in a quick breath, catching again that faint, faint hint of his cologne, and realized that might not have been the best idea. The scent seemed to trigger all her nerve endings, bringing back the previous Friday night, the way his arms had gone around her, the feel of his lips on hers, somehow soft and strong and insistent all at the same time.

A shiver went over her, and she forced herself to look out the car window, to focus on the trees wheeling about them as Lucas turned the SUV around in the enormous driveway so they wouldn't have to back out onto the street.

"Everything okay?" he asked.

"Fine," she said. "Maybe a little hungry."

It was a now a few minutes past two; she'd had some soup and crackers before she left Jerome, but the light lunch didn't seem to be holding on very well. That could explain her current unsettled state.

"Well, I have a nice dinner planned for us, but that doesn't mean we can't get a snack while we're out. I know just the place."

She forced a smile. "Sounds great."

They wound their way down through his neighborhood, so much more orderly and well-manicured than anything you'd see in Jerome, and on past that to a much larger street that went through a commercial area, with the sorts of chain stores she guessed were common to most medium-sized towns. It was of course much busier than Cottonwood, where she did the majority of her shopping, and even busier than Sedona, which was choked with tourists most of the time. And yet, in the grand scheme of things, Flagstaff wasn't really that large a town. Out of curiosity, she'd looked it up once. Sixty thousand and some change. Nothing compared to Phoenix or Los Angeles or New York, but still an order of magnitude bigger than tiny Jerome.

At least the downtown area, once they got there, felt more familiar, most likely because many of the buildings were of the same vintage as those in Jerome. She'd come up on Tuesday, to avoid the weekend crowds, but it still felt congested to her, and they ended up having to leave the BMW in a subter-ranean structure, as no street parking was available.

"This way," Lucas said, once they emerged on the street level.

She noticed he was careful not to reach out and take her by the hand, but instead pointed in the direction they needed to go. At that moment, she actually would have welcomed his holding her hand, simply because the wind had picked up and had a definite bite to it, chilling her fingers. She'd brought gloves with her, but she hadn't thought she would need them on a sunny afternoon. Flagstaff looked so much warmer than it actually was.

But since they set a brisk pace, she found it wasn't so bad, and before long they were taking a shortcut down an alley to a sort of outdoor mall with shops and restaurants. Lucas led her into the first restaurant, which turned out to be a tapas place, one Margot thought she'd heard Angela mention once or twice. The food had sounded delicious, but Margot had certainly never thought she would get the opportunity to eat there.

It was a seat-yourself kind of establishment, so they chose a table by the window and sat down. At this time of day, after lunch but before happy hour, it was deserted except for the wait staff.

"It's two o'clock on a weekday," Lucas said, dark eyes twinkling at her over the top of his menu. "Is that late enough for drinking sangria or not?"

He really wasn't ever going to let her live that remark down. "It's afternoon," she replied calmly, "so I think it's safe. Although I do wonder why you'd want to drink something cold when it's barely fifty degrees outside."

A quick grin. "Once you've had a glass, you'll know why."

The waiter came over then, and Lucas ordered two glasses of sangria, along with some bacon-wrapped dates. "We'll take it easy at first," he told her, once the waiter had gone. "That's the fun thing about tapas—you can just keep ordering different ones until you feel full."

"I thought you said you had something special planned for dinner."

"I do, so scratch the 'full' comment. Let's go for 'moderately satisfied.'"

She could only shake her head at that, and watch as he poured her some water from the carafe on the table. Since she'd forgotten to bring along any bottled water for the drive, she was fairly thirsty at this point, and gratefully accepted the glass from him when he handed it to her.

"I do appreciate you coming here, Margot," he said then, his expression quite serious. "I know it's a big step."

Was it? She'd been trying to play it safe, think of this as…what, a fact-finding mission? A way to step outside the boundaries she'd set for herself all these years? Not because she wanted to spend time with him. The thing was, she knew she did. She liked talking to him, especially if they weren't sparring over her refusal to admit that an elder couldn't be allowed much of a personal life.

Oh, who was she kidding? Yes, she liked talking to him...but she also liked looking at him. Way, way more than she should. And she wasn't going to let herself think about what it had been like to kiss him.

"It's—" She'd been about to say that it was nothing, but they both knew that was a lie, didn't they? "Thank you for having me."

In that moment, the gleam returned to his eyes, and she realized she'd stuck her foot in it with that comment. Yes, she was sure he would be more than glad to "have" her.

To her relief, the waiter came back with their glasses of sangria in that moment, and Margot was able to cover her embarrassment by taking a long sip of the drink through its straw. Lucas hadn't been exaggerating; it was marvelous. Who cared that it was more hot chocolate weather outside?

"What do you think?" he asked.

I think I've been missing out my whole life. Of course she would never say such a thing out loud, so she only replied, "It's amazing."

"I hope Flagstaff will continue to amaze you."

She had a feeling it would, if Lucas Wilcox had anything to do about it.

There was something slightly surreal about being here and realizing it was Margot Emory sitting opposite him, right in the middle of his hometown, smack in the center of Wilcox territory…and that she didn't look out of place at all. He loved watching her, seeing the way her dark hair slipped over her shoulders, watching the way the little amulet at her throat—was that Angela's work?—twinkled in the light.

She looked like she belonged here. And God, did he want her to belong here. Hadn't Jerome had enough of her already?

"…around here?" she was saying, and Lucas blinked.

"Sorry, what?"

Her dark eyes narrowed slightly, and he wondered if she could guess what he had been thinking. He hoped not; he was trying the best he could to be casual and suave about all this, and let her form her own conclusions…make her own decisions. "I was asking if Connor's gallery is around here."

"Actually, it is." Lucas pointed at the window in the direction of the alley. "That brick building there with the green door? The gallery is in the front half on the ground floor, and then his apartment was the one directly above on the right. The other apartment he used as his studio. It's still empty because it needs a lot of renovation before it's fit for actual occupation."

"So he can rent it out to another cousin?"

"Probably," he replied, somewhat surprised she knew that much of the arrangements they'd made. Then again, Margot was an elder, and so Angela must have consulted with her a good bit as to her plans.

"Makes sense," Margot remarked. "I'm guessing you must have a goodly number of cousins who need lodging."

"A fair number." Actually, he'd never really stopped to count, but there were hundreds and hundreds of Wilcoxes in the Flagstaff area. Marie was the one who really kept track of that sort of thing. "I'd imagine those sorts of logistics would even be harder in Jerome."

A rueful smile touched her mouth before she sipped some more sangria. ""That's an understatement. There's not a lot of real estate to go around, obviously. It's led to people being pretty fanatical about their wills, just so there's no confusion when it comes time for a property to be handed down." She paused, her expression faraway and a little sad. Lucas wondered if she was thinking about her own single state, and who her own cottage might go to someday. But then she straightened in her chair and added, "We've managed, though. Our territory is nowhere big as yours, of course, but there's still plenty of room for us to spread out in Cottonwood and Clarkdale and Camp Verde."

"Or Prescott," Lucas ventured, then wanted to kick himself. Wasn't her asshole of an ex-fiancé from Prescott?

If he hadn't been watching for it, he probably wouldn't have even noticed the slight hesitation before she said, "Yes, there's a small branch of the family over there, too."

The waiter came by with the bacon-wrapped dates then, and Lucas tried to prevent himself from letting out a sigh of relief at the welcome interruption. He waited as Margot selected a date and put it on her own small plate, then took one for himself. Her reaction was all he could have hoped for; she carefully cut the morsel in half, then put one piece in her mouth. Almost at once, her dark lashes swept down over her eyes as she appeared to savor the bite.

"Good?"

"That's—" She broke off, seeming to consider the perfect word to use, and said, "Decadent."

That sounded about right to him. "Yes, they are that."

The two of them were quiet for a minute or two, demolishing the rest of the dates in short order. Margot's glass of sangria was about three-quarters gone, while Lucas knew he was about to start making rude noises with his straw if he attempted to get any more out of the bottom of his glass.

"Another one?" he asked.

"I think I'm good," she replied. "We're going to be walking a good bit, so it's probably better if I'm not completely tipsy."

Actually, he thought the extra bit of muscle relaxant might do her some good, but he knew better than to tell her that. "Anything else you'd like to eat?"

She smiled at him. It was a genuine smile, one without any irony or sarcasm in it. "No, that was perfect. Just enough to take the edge off. Thank you."

It definitely had taken the edge off. She seemed more relaxed now, not so worried about what he had planned or what was coming next. He took that as a good sign. So he signaled the waiter that they were ready for the check, and within a few minutes, they were back outside, the fresh breeze playing with the ends of Margot's hair, making her push it back impatiently.

"We can cut down this alley," Lucas said, leading her to the narrow lane that separated Connor's building from the restaurant across from the tapas place.

She followed him, looking around with some interest, although truthfully, there wasn't that much to see. It could be a little awkward in here if someone decided to come this way in their car, but luckily they made it through without incident, and veered to the left so they could enter the gallery.

Joelle was working, of course, and called out a "hi" to Lucas he came inside. Her gaze slid questioningly toward Margot, and he said hastily, "Joelle, this is Margot Emory. She's a cousin of Angela's."

"Oh, hi—nice to meet you!" Joelle chirped. She tended to be cheery all the time, which made things easier for Connor, as he wasn't exactly what you could call a good salesman. Although Joelle was a civilian, she knew there was something slightly different about the Wilcox family, although of course she didn't have many details. But she knew enough to realize that Lucas Wilcox having a cousin of Angela's as his companion was kind of a big deal.

"I'm just showing her around a bit," he explained, hoping she would get the hint and not be too inquisitive.

"Oh, sure, take a look around. Connor's not coming in today—I'm sure he'll be sorry that he missed you."

"It's fine," Lucas said hastily. The last thing he wanted was interruptions from any of his relatives, even one as hands-off as Connor. "I talked to him the day before yesterday." Which was sort of a non sequitur, but it did seem to get Joelle to back off.

"Great," she responded, and went back to knotting tiny price tags on threads, no doubt gearing up to prepare a new collection of local artisanal jewelry for the holiday buying season.

In the meantime, Margot had wandered a few paces away and was studying an abstract sculpture of dichroic glass and brazed brass tubing. From what he'd seen on the gallery walk with her, it didn't seem to be her kind of thing. He approached her and said, "Like it?"

She tipped her head to one side, her attention seeming to be completely focused on the piece. "I'm not sure yet. I'm trying to decide whether I do or not. It's interesting, though."

"Connor's trying to branch out, I think." There wasn't much more Lucas could say on the subject, as art—modern or otherwise—was not his field of expertise.

"It's a very nice gallery," she said. "Intimate, but not crowded. A good use of space."

"I'll pass your compliments on to Connor," Lucas said with a wry smile.

Her eyebrows went up, and then she gave a small laugh. "Oh, I suppose that sounds as if I was critiquing it or something. I just meant that it's very nice."

"'Nice' works."

They spent another five minutes or so poking around, and then he led her back outside, where the afternoon had started to look somewhat darker. Clouds were beginning to pile up to the northeast, moving their way.

"Is it going to rain?" Margot asked, following his gaze.

"I doubt it. Nothing's been forecast. But I was thinking about taking you up to the observatory, so we might as well head straight there in case it gets too cloudy to see anything."

She nodded, and followed him as he led her back to the parking structure. Normally he didn't pay much attention to the weather, except to make sure he'd have a clear day for playing golf. Now, though, he cast a wary eye toward the sky, and wondered if Mother Nature had decided to throw a monkey wrench into his plans.

Then again, if the weather did get really bad, he could think of worse things than being trapped in his house with Margot Emory for a few days….

CHAPTER EIGHT

THE WHOLE TIME THEY WERE AT LOWELL OBSERVATORY, the clouds moved in slowly, inexorably. It stayed dry, however, and since they were really there to tour the grounds and see a couple of the presentations, it didn't matter much that the day had become so overcast. Lucas had told her the staff at Lowell did solar observations right at noon, but since they'd gotten to the site sometime after four, that didn't affect Lucas and Margot's plans.

Afterward, they drove back to his house. It was now past six-thirty, and the sun had already set. Margot was somewhat surprised that they hadn't headed back downtown for dinner, but she decided to roll with it. After all, Lucas had told her he had something special planned for dinner, so he obviously knew what he was doing. Maybe he did expect her to change so they could go back out someplace that required a bit more dressing up than jeans and a sweater, although from what she'd seen so far today, the populace of Flagstaff rivaled Jerome's in terms of utter casualness. She'd noticed that Lucas had sent a text right before they got in the car to leave the observatory parking lot; maybe he was confirming a reservation or something.

They pulled into the driveway, and she immediately saw the white van parked off to one side, where it wouldn't block any of the garage bays. "Friend of yours?" she inquired, nodding toward the vehicle.

"Something like that," he said easily. "You'll see."

He pulled into the garage and turned off the engine, and they both got out and headed into the house. When they entered the kitchen, Margot stopped dead in shock. A man and a woman were at work there, putting together what clearly looked like quite an elaborate dinner.

"Lucas?" she asked.

He grinned. "I said I had something special planned for dinner. I thought it would be more fun to eat in, but as I didn't want to poison you, I had Jeff and Claire come in to do the heavy lifting."

"Good call," the man—Jeff—said. "Considering he can barely fry an egg." He returned his attention to Lucas and added, "Give us about fifteen minutes."

"No problem."

Somewhat bemused, Margot followed Lucas out of the kitchen and past the dining room, where she saw the table had already been set with gleaming warm-toned china and glittering crystal. She looked up at him. "You do think of everything, don't you?"

"I try to." He didn't wait for her to reply, but went on, "We have a little time. I don't expect you to dress for dinner or anything, but if you want to freshen up a bit—"

"I do." Actually, she thought dressing for dinner sounded like a good idea. That table was far too elegant for jeans and a simple sweater. "I'll be back down in few minutes."

"Sounds good."

As she went up the stairs, she wondered if changing would make it look as if she were trying too hard. After all, Lucas seemed to be fine with staying in his own jeans and sweater. But she'd packed those dresses, and she figured she might as well get some use out of them.

Fifteen minutes actually went by fairly quickly when you had to change your entire outfit, touch up your makeup, brush your hair, and give everything a once-over before heading back downstairs. Margot eyed herself quickly, hoping she didn't look too "done." But it wasn't as if she'd put on a cocktail dress or something—she wore a black maxi dress with some color around the neck and hem, a necklace of coral and turquoise resting on her collarbone. Her boots did have heels, but they weren't strappy sandals, and so she hoped Lucas would take her effort for what it was, which was wanting to look nice at dinner but not in anything overtly sexy.

Amazing smells were drifting up from the kitchen as she descended the stairs once more, and she entered the dining room to find Lucas opening a bottle of wine. As he looked up from the wine, she could see his dark eyes glow with admiration. So much for being low-key about dressing up.

He didn't say anything at first, however, as if sensing that a compliment was not something she'd welcome in that moment. Once he had the cork extricated from the bottle, he did remark, "Perfect timing. Claire and Jeff are just about ready. Why don't you go ahead and take a seat?" He pointed at the chair immediately to the right of the one at the head of the table.

"They're not going to serve us, are they?" she asked, thinking that was expecting a bit much.

"No, we're not," Claire said smartly as she brought in a bowl of mixed field greens. "Just bringing everything out and letting you sort it from there."

Margot summoned a faint smile as Claire returned to the kitchen, passing Jeff, who had another bowl in his hands, this one of what smelled like garlic mashed potatoes. He set it down, and they did their little dance once again, this time with her carrying a very large bowl of some kind of beef dish, judging by the savory aroma, and Jeff bringing out a basket of bread, carefully covered with a brick-red napkin.

"That's it, then," he said to Lucas. "Everything's cleaned up. We want to hit the road—that storm coming in looks bad."

"It does?" Lucas said, apparently taken off guard by this revelation.

"Well, according to the alert I just got on my weather app, it does. Have a great dinner—*bon appetit!*"

With that he ducked back into the kitchen, and Lucas, after a short pause, went ahead and took his seat next to her. He picked up the bottle of wine and poured a measure into her glass, then his.

"Is the storm going to be a problem?" she asked.

At once he smiled and shook his head. "I doubt it. I didn't see much on the news this morning, and besides, even if it does do something crazy and actually snow—which generally doesn't happen this early in November—I'm sure it'll be melted by morning."

"And if it doesn't melt?" She wasn't sure she believed him. What would happen if they really did get snowed in here? Sure, they had food for tonight— well, the next several days, judging by the size of the meal Claire and Jeff had prepared—but it didn't sound as if Lucas was the type to keep much in the way of supplies around.

He seemed to recognize her concern, replying, "If it doesn't…well, I wasn't sure if you were much of a 'going out to breakfast' person, based on the way you shot down my suggestion about having brunch that one time, so I did get a few things. It'll be fine."

His reply did allow her to relax…a little. It was one thing to be up here in Flagstaff, running around town and doing things in public. What was she supposed to do if she really did get trapped in Lucas' house for several days because they were snowed in?

Relax, she told herself. *It's Flagstaff in the twenty-first century, not something out of Little House on the Prairie. Even if we do get a heavy snowstorm, I'm sure the roads will be plowed in no time.*

"Okay," she allowed, and he raised his glass to her. Uncertainly, she did the same.

He said, "To trying new things."

She wasn't sure how she was supposed to respond to that particular toast, but she knew it would be rude if she didn't chime in. And really, just being here in Flagstaff, in Wilcox territory, was a new enough thing for her. She wouldn't worry about what Lucas might or might not have meant.

"To trying new things."

They clinked glasses and then drank. It was a Rhone-style blend, she thought, although she knew there was no way she'd be able to tell if it was a true Rhone wine or one of the blends whipped up by the mad geniuses at one of the Verde Valley's various wineries. Either way, it was marvelous, rich and nuanced, yet not too heavy on the tannins.

She set her glass down. "That's excellent."

"I'm glad you like it—it's one of your own."

"Mine?"

A smile. "From Burning Tree Cellars. They're in McAllister territory, right? So I guess I think of the winery as being yours."

Margot supposed that was true, if you stopped to think about it. "I had no idea you'd been coming down there and shopping regularly."

"Oh, I haven't. Connor picked this up for me the last time he was there, told me he was really impressed with their blends and that he thought I'd appreciate them, too."

"And do you?"

The dark eyes surveyed her over the rim of his wine glass. "Oh, yes. Definitely."

Once again she got the feeling he was discussing something entirely different from what she had asked, but she decided to let it go.

He seemed to as well, setting down his glass so he could hand her the bowl of salad. She took some, waited for him to help himself, then took a bite. The dressing was a light vinaigrette, expertly balanced.

"So do Jeff and Claire run a restaurant, or do they just do freelance cooking around town for men trying to impress their dates?" Damn. Why had she said "date"? That was going to sound all wrong.

Judging by the way one corner of his mouth quirked, she guessed Lucas had picked up on the word right away. "They own a restaurant. But Tuesday's a slow night, so I wooed them away for a few hours while their *sous chefs* handled things."

Margot didn't want to think what that had cost. But it was pretty obvious that Lucas had enough money to do just about anything he wanted, so she wouldn't even bother to protest that he shouldn't have gone to so much trouble for her.

"Very impressive," she said, returning to her salad, keeping her eyes on her food so she wouldn't have to meet his.

He made a noncommittal sound and applied himself to his own salad. When they were both done, he rose and took her empty plate, then his, and disappeared briefly into the kitchen. She hadn't really planned it that way, but she was staring in the direction he'd gone, so when he came back to the dining room, their eyes met for the briefest second. Warmth flooded through her at that gaze, and at once she looked back down, pretending to be rear-ranging the napkin on her lap.

Why the hell did he have such an effect on her? The way Lucas made her feel seemed worlds away from the way she had reacted to Clay.

But no, she wouldn't think about that. She managed to smile as Lucas asked for her plate so he could dish up some potatoes and beef bourgignon for her, murmur a polite thank-you, and then wait while he got some for himself.

"I figured this was safe, since you had the venison at Rene's," he ventured, and she blinked, then realized he was talking about the food.

"Oh, yes. It's fine. I mean, it smells marvelous."

He nodded, and they both ate in silence for a minute or two. At last he said, "You seem sort of tense, Margot."

Well, of course she was. She was sitting here with him at his dining room table, by candlelight. Most women would have been thrilled to have a man take so much trouble to create a memorable evening like this. But she didn't know how to react to it. Should she remain coolly polite, letting him know that candles and Rhone wine and meals home-cooked by five-star chefs were all well and good, but that she had more backbone than to fall for something like that?

Or should she acknowledge that his efforts made some part of her feel all warm and melting, because it had been forever and a day since someone had paid this kind of attention to her?

No, that wasn't true. Not really. No one had *ever* done anything like this for her before. Certainly not Clay.

"I suppose it's all a lot to take in." From somewhere she summoned a smile, along with the courage to meet his gaze directly. "I do appreciate all this. Really."

"Okay." After that, he seemed to let the matter drop, and moved on to talking about what they would do if it really did snow, how maybe he could take her up to the Snow Bowl and they could watch people playing in the snow, and then to a restaurant he knew of on the way there that wasn't pretentious at all, but had some amazing soups and sandwiches.

She nodded and said that sounded like it would be fun, but her response felt tinny in her ears, as if she were saying the things she thought she should be saying, and not the one that lay in the very depths of her soul, of her heart.

No, I want to stay here. I want to stand with you in the garden and have you kiss me and keep me warm while the snow falls all around us.

Of course she would never tell him such a thing.

It really wasn't fair that she should be so beautiful. In a way, her dress was almost prim, with its high collar, but the way it opened in front to reveal a glimpse of the heavy Navajo necklace she wore underneath, and a fainter glimpse still of the shadow between her breasts, seemed far more enticing than something that showed a lot more flesh would be.

Somehow Lucas managed to keep himself from staring at her, at the all too solid reality of her just a few feet away at his dining room table, but it wasn't easy. His mouth kept moving, uttering the sort of easy banter he could probably manage in his sleep if necessary, and all the while his brain kept thinking, I want you. *I want you. I want you.*

All right, it wasn't just his brain thinking that.

He had to force himself not to dwell on the curves of her body as revealed in the slim-fitting dress, because otherwise he'd have to force back an arousal for which there was no cure. Well, of course, there *was* a cure, but he didn't think Margot seemed too interested in providing it.

Or…was she? The signals he kept getting from her were so mixed that he honestly didn't know what to think. One minute she'd be polite, but only that, and in the next, her gaze would catch his, and he'd see a flicker of the same heat he knew rushed over his body every time he recalled that one sweet time he'd kissed her.

They talked of inconsequential things, of the possibility of snow, of how quickly the roads would be plowed, of the arrangements Connor and Angela had made in case the weather was not cooperating whenever the twins decided to make their entrance into the world. In that case, Darrell Wilcox, currently a junior at Northern Pines, would come out to make the trip with them. His talent, such as it was, involved making an area in front of him extremely hot. In most cases, it wasn't a lot of use—although Lucas suspected his cousin had given his siblings a hot foot a time or two—but Darrell did make an excellent impromptu snow plow.

And eventually they had eaten and drunk their fill, and Margot insisted on helping him clear the table. Since Jeff and Claire had tidied up all evidence of the actual meal preparations, it was short work to put the leftovers in storage containers and the dirty dishes in the dishwasher. Then Lucas straightened up, wondering what he could do to extend the evening. Margot really didn't seem like the type to watch television—he hadn't even seen a TV at her place—and she hadn't appeared terribly inclined toward conversation, at least not the sort of conversation he wanted, when she would unbend enough to reveal a little more about herself.

He saw Margot's gaze shift toward the kitchen door, which was basically a window in a doorframe, one that opened on the deck, and her eyes lit up. "I think—I think it's snowing!"

Thank God. Let it snow, he thought. *Let it snow like that one storm five years ago when it came up to the windows. Then we'll be trapped in here together, and she'll have no choice but to finally open up.*

"Let's take a look," he said, hoping he sounded more or less unconcerned. He dried his hands on a dish towel and went to the door, then opened it.

A blast of freezing air entered the warm kitchen, but Margot didn't seem to mind. The lights mounted on the rear of the house had turned on automatically at dusk, and so it was easy to see the pale flakes floating down, dancing this way and that. They were falling fast, too, and thickly, so much so that he could see the snow already beginning to pile up on the deck railings and the patio furniture, shrouded for the season, and on the boards of the deck itself.

"It's beautiful," she said quietly.

"I thought it snowed in Jerome sometimes."

"It does, but something about it here feels quieter, deeper. Maybe it's all the pine trees around the house."

He could see that. Yes, there were trees in Jerome, but nothing like the stately ponderosa pines that surrounded his home. A minute passed as they stood in silence, watching the snow fall, and then he said, "It's too cold to stand here like this. The last thing I want is you getting sick."

"I never get sick," she said absently, but she did step away from the door so he could close it, shutting out the falling snow and the icy air that had begun to penetrate even the wool sweater he wore.

"You'll still be able to see it if we go into the living room," he went on. "All those windows look out over the deck, too."

She nodded, and he led her out of the kitchen, on to the big chamber where the fireplace already had logs piled in it, waiting for just this moment. Well, he hadn't thought it would really snow, but you didn't need snow to want a fire on a cold evening in November. Since he didn't have Margot's facility for sparking off a fire whenever she felt like it, he had to settle for using a long-necked butane lighter to get the logs going. In a few minutes, they were crackling away cheerily.

As he tended the fire, she moved to the windows so she might stand there and watch the snow coming down, thicker and thicker, so you could begin to see the waves and ripples in it. That seemed to him a sign that the snow wasn't planning on going away anytime soon, and he sent a mental thanks heavenward for the storm and its unexpected strength. He recalled something else, too, and went to a small cabinet in a corner of the room, extracting a pair of heavy blown-glass shot glasses before pouring a good measure of cognac into each one.

"For the cold," he said, handing one to Margot.

For the barest second, she hesitated, and then she took it from him. "I did get a little chilled," she admitted.

"Then *skoal*," he said, and they clinked their glasses and took a sip. The cognac pulsed down his throat, warm and welcome, although he noticed that Margot winced a bit as she swallowed. Probably not used to the strong stuff.

"What do you do when it gets like this?" she asked, and he shrugged.

"Wait it out. I said I didn't cook, but it's not as if I don't keep stuff on hand just in case. Watch TV. Surf the Internet, as long as the cable doesn't crap out or the electricity go out."

She looked vaguely alarmed. "Does that happen often?"

"Hardly ever. We're used to getting pounded in this city, so the infrastructure is built to take it. Besides, I have a generator out in the shed in case of a real emergency."

That answer seemed to satisfy her, as she inclined her head slightly and allowed herself another sip of cognac. This time she didn't shudder, which Lucas took as a good sign.

For the longest moment, she stood there, saying nothing, only watching the snow fall. Already the patio furniture and the barbecue in their winter covers had taken on vaguely threatening shapes, the accumulating snowflakes obscuring their true nature, making them look like monstrous huddled forms.

"Lucas," Margot said at last. Something in her tone made a chill run down his spine, a chill that had nothing to do with the cold air he could feel faintly seeping in past the French doors.

He kept his voice as calm as he could. "What?"

"What happens if I let myself trust you?"

"You don't trust me now?"

"You know what I mean."

Without replying, he plucked the shot glass from her hand and led her over to the sofa, the one that faced the fireplace. He set both their glasses down on the heavy copper-topped cocktail table, then said, "Do you think I'm anything like Clay McAllister?"

A short, bitter laugh. "No."

"Then why do you think I would treat you the same way?"

Her hands knotted in her lap. She wore a single coral ring on the middle finger of her right hand, but nothing else—no watch, no bracelet. He found he liked that, as her hands were slender and lovely, just like her, and didn't need any other embellishment.

"I don't know." Her eyes were fixed on the fire. So she wouldn't have to look at him. In that moment, he didn't care, if it meant she might go on talking. "I guess because I've sort of gotten out of the habit of trusting people. Men, I mean." She leaned forward and took one deliberate sip of her cognac before setting the glass back on the table. "Oh, that doesn't sound right, either. It's not like there was anyone after Clay."

"No one?" Lucas asked, startled. She couldn't possibly mean that she hadn't been with a single person since her ex-fiancé dumped her. Or...could she?

Something of what he'd been thinking must have revealed itself on his face, because she slanted a sardonic sideways glance at him up through her eyelashes. "No relationships, I mean. Not much else, either. About four years ago, I was feeling a bit... pent-up...if you know what I mean. So I went into Sedona, and the film festival was going on. It was February. I met some guy who said he was a producer and that I had a great look. Maybe he really was, but I still could recognize a line when I heard one. Not that it mattered. I wasn't looking for anything permanent. We both scratched our itch, and I went home to Jerome, and he went back to L.A., I suppose."

She spoke coolly, as if the whole thing had happened to someone else, but Lucas noticed that she'd returned to watching the fireplace, as if she didn't want to meet his eyes and find out how disappointed he was in her. Disappointment was probably the last thing he was feeling, though. Startled? Sure. Despite her cracks about casual sex the other day, he hadn't thought she could let go of herself enough to be with someone she didn't know. Or maybe that was exactly what she needed. Someone who didn't have a clue about who—or what—she was, didn't know her family history, didn't know anything except that she was an available and attractive woman.

"You do what you have to do," Lucas said, making sure his tone was completely neutral, with no hint of condemnation. "I don't think anyone would fault you for what happened in Sedona—although some people might question why you only did it once."

At that comment, she shifted on the couch so she was facing him. Her expression was hard to read. Maybe the tiniest bit confused? Then her lips twisted into a half-smile. "It took me enough effort to work up the nerve for that one time. And afterward…." A lift of the shoulders. "I wasn't too happy with what I'd done. So I guess I just stopped thinking about that part of myself. It was easier that way."

"And now?"

Her eyelids dropped, and she seemed to hesitate. "I don't know, Lucas. Everything you've done for me so far—it's incredible, and I know I should trust you, because I know Angela thinks the world of you, and she definitely doesn't feel that way about everyone. And you've been such a gentleman—"

"Except now," he murmured, his instincts telling him to reach out and pull her to him now, to bring his mouth to hers, taste the lingering warmth of the cognac on her lips, and beneath that some indefinable sweetness which was simply her.

He felt no resistance from her, which was what he'd feared, even as he let himself kiss her. No, she opened her mouth to him, tasted him as well, pressed herself against him, and suddenly she was beneath him on the couch, her body lithe and eager, so warm, and he ran one hand ran over her, finding the curve of her breast....

And then he felt her push against him, heard her gasp, "Lucas, I can't—"

At once he forced himself upright, giving her some distance so she could struggle to a sitting position. "Jesus, Margot, I'm sorry. I would never force you—"

Her mouth, now looking a little swollen, shaped itself into a rueful smile. "You weren't forcing me. I wanted—anyway, I just think it's too soon. I can't...I won't go there yet."

That was more than he'd hoped for. She had said "yet," after all. Not "no." He could wait. His body groaned at the delay, but his mind told it to get stuffed. "It's fine, Margot. I understand."

She nodded, then stood up. "I should probably go to bed now. Thank you for a lovely evening." A pause, as if she were deciding what she should do next. Then she went up on her tiptoes and kissed him on the cheek, and even that faint touch of her lips to his skin was enough to get his blood racing all over again.

His hands wanted to reach out to her, to pull her close, but he willed himself to stand still, to simply say, "You're welcome. Sleep well."

Another nod, and then she was gone, heading up the staircase to her room. Lucas stood in front of the fire for a long moment, body still throbbing with need, then let out a sigh as he went to bank down the fire.

If only his own emotions could be so easily controlled.

CHAPTER NINE

MARGOT WOKE EVEN EARLIER THAN USUAL, OPENING HER eyes and blinking at the faint half-light of pre-dawn. For a second or two, she couldn't recall where she was, didn't recognize the high ceiling or the long drapes at the window, so different from the wooden blinds in her own house. Then she realized she was sleeping in Lucas Wilcox's home, and that he was just a door or two down the hall from her.

And with that realization came the recollection of the way he had kissed her the night before, of how solid and strong his body had felt pressed against hers. He could never know how close she'd come to not stopping him. In fact, now she was regretting that she had. Wouldn't that be the best way to deal with the situation? Just let her emotions go for once, no matter what happened?

Even if nothing ultimately came of it, at least she'd have had one spectacular lay.

But her brain had put on the brakes, and so she was lying here alone, and not next to Lucas.

Damn it.

Scowling, she shoved back the bedclothes and went to the window, pushed the curtains aside so she could see what the storm had wrought. Although she was wearing a long-sleeved sleep shirt, she could feel the cold seeming to emanate from the very glass itself, and she wondered what the temperature must be outside. Way below freezing, that was for sure.

The world in every direction had been blanketed in white, the branches of the trees drooping with snow, the deck half buried. Across the pristine expanse of the backyard, Margot could see one set of prints marring the snow. Deer, maybe?

She glanced at the clock. Ten minutes after six. Well, she was up, so she figured she might as well take a shower and get ready for the day. She had no idea whether Lucas was a late or an early riser, and her cheeks heated a bit as she thought how she would now know the answer to that question if she'd only allowed things to progress to their logical conclusion the night before. He did play golf. She had a vague idea that golfers tended to get up early.

Well, whether he was an early riser or not, she still needed to get herself put together. Somehow it seemed as if it would be easier to face him with her makeup on and her hair done, so she went into the bathroom and turned on the water in the shower, impressed by how quickly it got hot. The same process would've taken twice as long with the balky water heater in her cottage.

But she wasn't going to start comparing apples and oranges. No, she'd just stand here and let the hot water run over her, rinsing away some of last night's encounter, allowing her to focus on the start of a new day. It did feel good, so she lingered there longer than she normally would, until at last she began to feel guilty about the water she was using up. No doubt this modern and up-to-date house could handle two people bathing at once, but she didn't want to risk Lucas having a lukewarm shower whenever he did get up.

She got out of the shower, dried off, climbed into her underwear, and went to choose her clothes for the day. It seemed fairly clear that they wouldn't be going anywhere soon, and so she put on a new pair of jeans and another sweater, this one a dark purple. After that it was time to dry her hair and put on some makeup, and by that point she felt more or less ready to face the world...or at least Lucas Wilcox.

The house felt quiet, calm, as she opened her door and went out into the hall. No sign of Lucas, not even the distant whispery sound of a shower running, and she hesitated for a moment. Would it seem odd to be roaming around the house when he wasn't even up? But she could use some tea, if he had any. And maybe she'd grab the little sketchpad from her purse and try her hand at a rendering of all those tall pines blanketed with snow. It would probably be a dismal failure, but at least it would give her something to do.

After fetching the sketchpad and a pencil, she went back out to the hall and then moved cautiously down the stairs. It felt colder here, and she wondered if the house had a dual-zone heating system. If it did, she certainly had no idea how to operate it. Well, getting some hot water going would help to warm up the kitchen at least.

She entered the kitchen, and set down the sketchpad and pencil on the counter. On the stovetop she spied a bright red kettle—empty, of course—and she picked it up, then filled it with water before replacing it on the back burner. To one side of the refrigerator was the pantry, so she opened one of the doors, hoping she'd be able to find some tea. She didn't spy any at first, but she did see canned beans and cunning little packets of pre-made sauces, so at least they wouldn't completely starve if they did end up trapped here for a while. One cupboard over, she finally found a brand-new box of Darjeeling, still with the cellophane wrapper on it.

Despite herself, she smiled. How had Lucas known that was her favorite? She couldn't recall ever mentioning it to him.

A bit more exploration led her to locate a nice sturdy mug of what looked like hand-fired and hand-painted earthenware. She wondered if it was the work of a local artisan, possibly someone in the Wilcox clan. It felt smooth and sturdy under her fingers, and she set it on the counter as she opened the box of tea and then dropped a bag into the mug.

A minute later, the kettle began to whistle. She lifted it from the burner as quickly as she could, since she really didn't want to wake Lucas up if he still was asleep. Pausing, she listened, but didn't hear anything. Not that that necessarily meant much; in a house this big, would she even hear him moving around?

With a shrug, she poured the hot water over the tea bag, then went to peer out the glass door that overlooked the deck. All was quiet, the skies overcast, the air completely still. She retrieved the sketchpad and flipped to a fresh page, taking her pencil and roughing in the tall, slender shapes of the trees, the deck railings blunted by snow. The trees weren't so difficult, but she couldn't quite get the snow-topped railings right. They kept looking like flattened marshmallows.

"You never told me you were an artist."

She started and glanced over her shoulder. Lucas stood a few feet away, fully dressed, although his hair still looked a little damp. His jaw was dusted with dark stubble, which meant he probably hadn't shaved.

"I'm not an artist," she said carefully, closing the sketchpad. "Connor's an artist. I just like to draw things."

He came around the kitchen island and plucked the pad from her fingers before she could protest, then flipped it back open to the sketch she'd been working on. "It's good."

"No, it's not. It's just doodling."

With a grin, he said, "Margot, the weird loops and squiggles I put on the pad by the phone when I'm talking to someone are doodles. This is way beyond that."

While a part of her enjoyed hearing the praise, another was more than a little irritated by the way he'd just taken the sketchpad without so much as a by-your-leave. "I don't think so, but you're entitled to your opinion."

"Thank you. And my opinion is that you're good." He handed the sketchpad back to her and headed over to where the coffeemaker sat. "I see you found the tea."

"I did," she replied, recalling that it was probably past time to pull the tea bag out of the mug. She hurried over and began to extract it, then paused.

"The trash is under the sink," Lucas offered, clearly guessing the reason for her hesitation.

"Thanks." As she disposed of the used-up bag, he went to the refrigerator and pulled out a quart of milk. "Do you doctor your tea as badly as you do coffee?"

"Not quite to that extreme, but yes, I do take milk." She approached him, and he extended the carton to her. Maybe it was an accident, or maybe it was on purpose, but his fingers brushed against hers as she took it, and a little thrill went through her.

Ignoring that unwelcome *frisson*, she poured some milk into her tea, then asked, "Sugar?"

"Far left side of the pantry."

As Margot fetched it, he busied himself with getting the coffeemaker going. The domesticity of the scene just seemed to underscore for her how odd the situation was. They'd kissed, but they certainly hadn't slept together. Was this a date...an assignation...a friendly sleepover? She had no idea anymore.

She cleared her throat. "Do you think the roads are plowed yet?"

He slanted an amused glance in her direction. "What, planning a quick getaway?"

"No," she said at once. "That is, I was just curious."

The coffeemaker began chugging away, and the thick, rich scent of percolating coffee filled the kitchen. If only it tasted as good as it smelled.

"It's still pretty early, so I don't know if they've made it out here yet. Main priorities are the major streets, obviously." He leaned against the counter and glanced out the window. "Of course, it's sort of a moot point if I don't get the snowblower out on the driveway."

The idea of Lucas Wilcox trundling a snow-blower up and down his lengthy driveway was so amusing that she barely held in a chuckle. "You, with a snowblower?"

"Well, if I don't do it, who will? I'll admit my cousin Darrell is in pretty high demand on days like today, but his parents obviously have first priority. Besides, they live way at the other end of town, so I doubt he'd be able to get here any time soon. I don't mind blowing snow. It's kind of relaxing."

"Can I watch?" she asked, after taking a sip of tea.

"If it amuses you," he replied. He was smiling, but the way the dark eyes seemed to reach across the room and connect with hers told Margot that he wasn't entirely casual about the whole thing.

"I've just never seen anyone use one before. The main road in Jerome is always plowed because they have to keep the highway open all the time, and besides, even when we do get snow, it's only a few inches most of the time. Nothing that can't be handled with a shovel."

He gave a mock-shudder. "I don't even want to think about tackling that driveway with a shovel."

She couldn't really blame him for that. It was a very big driveway. But first things first. He couldn't take on that driveway, even armed with a snowblower, on an empty stomach. "I saw you were doing okay for canned goods. What about breakfast? I can make us some eggs and toast or something, if you've got the supplies."

"Anything you could possibly want," he replied, and opened the refrigerator so she could get a good look inside. And he was right—she saw several cartons of eggs, a package of bacon, another one of ham, and yet another of sausage. She lifted an inquiring eyebrow at him, and he added, somewhat apologetically, "I wasn't sure which one you liked best, so I got all of them."

"Okay, now I'm really not worried about starving." She considered a moment, then said, "Let's do the ham, if that's okay. I haven't had it for a while, and bacon is so messy."

He fetched everything and brought it over to the stove. "I think I can manage the eggs—"

"It's fine," she cut in. "Weren't you just saying yesterday you didn't want to poison me with your cooking? But if you can take care of the toast—"

"Sure. Sourdough, wheat, or English muffins?"

She wanted to laugh, but settled for replying, "Sourdough? And are scrambled eggs okay?"

"Sure."

They both went to work—or at least, he put the loaf of sourdough near the toaster oven and then fetched the pans she needed. As she cracked the eggs into a bowl, she reflected that she could get used to this sort of cozy domesticity. Bustling around the kitchen with Lucas was certainly more enjoyable than her lonely ritual of toast and tea…and although she couldn't deny that he was good to look at pretty much all the time, there was something about the way he looked in the morning, with his hair not combed all the way and his fine jaw shadowed with just enough stubble to enhance the strong bones rather than obscure them.

Once everything was done, they sat down with their food on the barstools that lined one edge of the bilevel kitchen island. Lucas took a bite of his eggs and let out a sigh. "So, are all you McAllister witches good cooks?"

"Scrambled eggs aren't that difficult, Lucas."

"You'd be surprised. I may or may not have killed a pan or two in the pursuit of decent scrambled eggs."

She chuckled. "Well, you do have to pay attention. As to your question, I have no idea, since I'm a long way from sampling everyone's cooking. But I'll admit that everything we put out at our Thanksgiving get-together is very good."

Looking thoughtful, he remarked, "I'd wrangle an invitation from Angela, but she's obviously staying put up here for Thanksgiving this year."

"Well, you could go with me," Margot said, surprising herself. Where the hell had that come from?

Apparently she wasn't the only one who was surprised, because he replied, his tone gently teasing, "Are you really willing to plan something with me a whole two weeks in advance?"

She glanced over at him. They were sitting side by side, probably not even a foot apart, and she'd been doing what she could to ignore that dangerous proximity the whole time she'd been eating breakfast. Maybe it had still played with her mind, getting her to make an offer she knew she shouldn't have. His eyes met hers, and her heart gave a painful little thump.

How long was she going to keep pretending?

Not very, it seemed. "Yes, I am," she said, speaking so quietly the words were barely above a murmur.

A long pause. Then she felt his left hand brush along her right knee, and a shiver went through her. "I can't tell you how glad it makes me to hear you say that," he told her, his tone also quiet, but no less intent for all that.

Unsure how to react, she reached out and picked up her now-lukewarm mug of tea, then took a large swallow. "Well," she said, attempting to adopt a teasing tone and not sure how well she was doing, "I did tell you the other day that you'd started to wear me down."

"And that's all it is? You're just tired of fighting me?"

Her fingers suddenly felt cold, despite being wrapped around the mug, which was still faintly warm. "I think we both know it's more than that." Should she set the mug down? She was afraid that if she did, Lucas would reach out to her, and while some part of her wanted that, she still needed the fragile distance between them to tell her she still had some control of the situation.

He let out a breath. "I—Margot—"

Shaking her head, she cut in, "Can we just leave it there for now, Lucas? I mean, it's barely eight o'clock in the morning. I try not to make any huge life decisions before ten, most days."

Despite the tension between them, he actually laughed at that. "I'd say that's a pretty good policy. Okay, we'll revisit all this once we've really had a chance to let the caffeine kick in. In the meantime, that driveway's not going to blow itself."

She couldn't help herself—she laughed out loud as well, and Lucas stared at her for a second before he realized what he'd just said.

"You know what I mean."

"Of course I do. Well, it should still be interesting to watch you blow a driveway."

He sent her a pained look, but then he got off the barstool and took his plate over to the sink. As he reached for the faucet to turn on the water, she said,

"I'll take care of the dishes. I figure you're going to be busy enough this morning."

"That's for sure. I'll get suited up, and just come outside whenever you're done in here."

She nodded, then began with the washing-up as he left the kitchen, presumably to get "suited up," whatever that meant. Not quite ten minutes later, as she was putting the clean pans on the counter to air dry, she heard a metallic whirring outside, and knew Lucas had just started with the driveway.

After fetching her coat and gloves, she went outside. It looked like he'd shoveled the walkway before starting on the drive, but even so the footing was treacherous. She was glad her boots had rubber soles, or she would have been in even more trouble.

Stepping carefully, she made her way to the edge of the driveway. Lucas was in the middle, pushing a bright red contraption, snow pluming up and away from him so it could pile up far enough away from the drive that there would still be room if he had to do this all over again. Goggles protected his eyes, and a red and white ski hat was mashed down on his head. He wore what looked like rubber wading boots, and Margot wanted to laugh at the sight of him. Not exactly the debonair figure he usually cut, but she thought she loved him even more like this.

Then she went stock-still. "Loved?" Since when did she love him? She'd barely begun to admit that she liked him. It was hard enough accepting that she was attracted to him. But it was a huge jump from liking someone and being attracted to him to thinking you were in love with him. That you loved him.

You're not in love with him, she told herself severely. *You hardly know him.*

And whose fault was that?

She sighed, and although of course he couldn't have heard such a small sound over the noise of the snowblower, something made Lucas turn toward her and wave, then give a thumbs-up sign.

Why did he have to be so adorable?

Because it would look odd if she didn't, she lifted a hand, waving back and smiling. He paused, turning the snowblower down to a dull roar. "This is probably going to take me at least an hour," he called out to her. "I doubt you want to be standing out in the cold all that time."

"You are," she pointed out.

"Yeah, but I'm working up a sweat. It's not the same as standing still."

He had a point. "Okay, I'll just watch for a few minutes, and then I'll go back inside."

"Good idea." He ratcheted the blower back up and continued down the driveway, appearing to cut an open path in the dead center. As she watched, he disappeared around the curve, although she could still hear the blower at work. A few minutes later he came back, and she could see better that he was going in circles, working out from the middle, so all the snow he'd just blown would keep getting pushed farther and farther to the edge.

During that time, she felt the cold beginning to seep up into her boots, sending icy little tendrils all through her body, and she realized she couldn't stay out here much longer. She waited until Lucas was close enough to hear her, and then she called out, "I'm turning into a popsicle, so I think I'd better get inside."

He nodded and smiled, then went back to pushing the snowblower. It felt wrong to leave him outside, working, and go back into the welcoming warmth of the house, but there really wasn't much she could to help. At least he looked like he knew what he was doing.

Of course he does, she told herself as she went back up the front walk and climbed the steps to the porch. *He's lived in Flagstaff his entire life. He should be an expert at that sort of thing.*

Since her boots were caked with snow, she paused at the door, pulled them off, and banged them on the porch floor to get the worst of it off. Dangling them from one hand, she went inside, then noticed a rack there, apparently for depositing muddy or snowy shoes. So she left the boots there and padded into the entry in her stocking feet, feeling strange to be in the house without Lucas, and doubly odd to be doing it with no shoes on.

He hadn't really mentioned what she should do to amuse herself while he was busy. Yes, there was the TV back in the family room, but she'd never been much of one for television. She realized then, what with one thing or another, that she hadn't checked her phone since the afternoon before. Anything could have happened during that time.

With that thought to spur her, she hurried up the stairs to her room, where she'd left her phone charging on the dresser. She picked it up.

Nothing. No calls, no texts, no emails. Well, that wasn't entirely true. Her mother had forwarded her a stuffing recipe that she thought might be something fun to try at Thanksgiving. Sylvia loved stuffing. Margot hated it, and yet invariably got stuck on the stuffing squad year after year.

She didn't know whether to laugh or cry as she set the phone down on the dresser. So much for having to be on call, day in and day out. Had she manufactured a need where there was none, or was Lucas right? Had her duties as elder changed irrevocably once the Wilcoxes were no longer a threat?

Her brain didn't quite know what to do with that. She left the bedroom and paused in the hallway, hesitating. All of the doors along that corridor stood open, which seemed to indicate that Lucas didn't mind if she looked inside them. It wouldn't really be snooping, would it, if he'd given her tacit permission?

It felt like something of a gray area, but her feet seemed to propel her forward on their own volition. The room next to hers was clearly his home office, with built-in shelves and a big desk on which sat a silvery laptop, now closed. That room had more books in it than she would have expected of Lucas, who'd never seemed like much of a reader to her. She wouldn't poke through them now, although if the snow decided to kick back up again, she might be in search of reading material in the near future.

I'm sure Lucas would be more than happy to entertain you.

That thought made a flush rise to her cheeks, and she made herself keep going. Next to the office was a bathroom with the same tile and slate flooring as the one she'd been using. Opposite the bathroom was another bedroom, this one apparently also intended as a guest room, although smaller than the one where she was staying. A daybed with a cover in cheerful stripes of red and orange and blue and green sat up against one wall, and directly opposite was a low dresser. A painting that looked like one of Connor's hung over the dresser, its autumnal colors echoing the hues of the daybed cover, but that was the only furniture the room contained.

At the end of the hall was the master suite. Margot took the quickest peek inside, catching a glimpse of warm terra-cotta-painted walls and sturdy furniture similar to what was in the bedroom where she'd slept, although this set was darker in tone. The bed was large, and rumpled. Apparently Lucas hadn't bothered to make it before he came downstairs.

That was enough. She certainly wasn't going inside, and it already seemed as if she'd caught too intimate a glimpse of the space, with its unmade bed and the discarded shoes next to it. It was the first remotely messy thing she'd seen in the house, since everything else there was even tidier than her own cottage, but maybe he'd been in a hurry to come down and be with her.

Hoping for a repeat of last night? Possibly. Then again, he hadn't made a single move yet. Or maybe his thoughts didn't start running along those lines until later in the day.

She took in a breath, then made herself turn around and go back downstairs. From outside she could still hear the roar of the snowblower, so clearly Lucas wasn't done yet with the driveway. All right, then she'd head on back to the family room. Television wasn't something that interested her much, although she should be able to find something useful, like a weather report. The app on her phone could have supplied her with some of that information, but a live weather report would probably be more detailed.

Now that she had a plan, she went on into the family room, still in her stocking feet, and found the remote on the coffee table. Naturally, the television was still tuned to a sports station, but she surfed until she found a weather channel. They were talking about the weather on the East Coast, so she had to hope they'd eventually track westward and give some hint as to what might be happening next in Arizona.

In the meantime, she spied some photos sitting on one of the side tables that flanked the sofa, and went over to pick one up. It showed Lucas and an older woman with iron-gray hair cut in a chin-length bob. Their smiles were so identical that Margot guessed the woman must be his mother. Another photo showed a much younger Lucas and the same woman, this time with her dark hair as yet untouched by any gray. He looked so young that Margot wondered if the picture had been taken while he was still in college. His style was certainly far more casual than it was now—untucked flannel shirt, faded jeans.

"Snooping?" came his voice, clearly amused, and she turned around to see him standing in the doorway, holding the red and white ski cap in one hand and fluffing his hair with another.

"I'm sorry—I thought I'd try to check the weather, and I saw the photos—"

"It's okay," he replied with a grin. "If I didn't want people looking at them, I wouldn't have them sitting out, right?"

"I suppose so." She couldn't shake the feeling that she'd been doing something illicit. Or maybe it was just that she really had been snooping upstairs a few minutes ago. "Is that your mother?"

"Yes."

No pictures or mention of a father. Well, it wasn't as if she didn't have some experience of that. "Does she live close by?"

His expression clouded for just the briefest second, and then he shook his head, smile still in place. "No, she lives in Tusayan with her girlfriend. That's up by the Grand Canyon."

He said it in such an offhand way that at first the words didn't quite penetrate. Then, not knowing what else to say, she replied, "Oh." *Goddess, that sounded awful....*

Maybe she actually had winced, because Lucas gave a chuckle and went on, "It's fine. She's been out for about twenty years. Of course, it probably would've been better if she'd figured all that out *before* she married my father, but...." He trailed off, shrugging.

"And he's...?"

"Here in Flagstaff. He remarried a couple of years after the divorce, so I have two half-brothers and a half-sister and a whole bunch of nieces and nephews." His attention shifted to the television, where the forecasters were now discussing an early freeze in the South. "Any news on the weather? It's getting darker out there again."

"Not yet. I guess our part of the country is last on the list."

"Then I'm going to run up and take another quick shower, if you don't mind."

She gave him a quick look. Some of his hair was sticking to his forehead, and she could see a sheen of sweat on his skin. "I have a feeling I'd mind more if you didn't take a shower."

"Well, I definitely don't want to offend. I'll be back down in a bit."

He headed out after that, and Margot attempted to return her attention to the TV. For a moment she wondered if he'd been disturbed by her asking about his mother, but she didn't think so. He seemed to have taken the whole thing in stride, just as he did just about everything else.

She couldn't help wondering if she'd be able to answer his questions about her parents with the same aplomb, should the topic come up. Well, she'd just have to hope it didn't.

CHAPTER TEN

THE SHOWER FELT GOOD, BUT LUCAS WOULDN'T ALLOW himself to luxuriate in it. He was all too acutely aware of the woman waiting for him downstairs. He'd already lost an hour of her company dealing with that damn driveway—and if his lifetime here in Flagstaff told him anything, it was that the look of the skies indicated there would be more snow, and soon.

Oh, well.

He got out, scrubbed his hair dry, squinted at his reflection in the steamy mirror, and decided to blow off the shaving for today. In the past, he'd had women tell him they liked it when he looked a little scruffy, so he could only hope Margot had similar tastes.

The clothes he'd been wearing to clear the driveway certainly couldn't be worn again, so he chucked them in the hamper and pulled on some clean jeans and a flannel shirt. If the weather held, maybe he'd worry about putting on a sweater or something, but this should be fine for now.

A glance at the clock told him he'd only taken about fifteen minutes to shower and get dressed. Not too bad. But it still felt like time wasted.

When he returned to the family room, Margot still had the TV tuned to the weather, but you really didn't need the forecaster's blather to tell you that the storm had decided to park itself over Flagstaff for a while. Outside the window, fat white flakes of snow had begun to fall again.

Margot must have noticed his pained glance outside, because she said, "I'm sorry about the driveway."

"It's all right. As they say, it's better to blow six inches twice than twelve inches once."

Her mouth twitched, and he grinned.

"Margot Emory, you have a dirty mind."

"I do not," she protested. "I think you have a dirty mind for thinking that *I* have a dirty mind."

"Fair enough." He came and sat down on the couch next to her, and he couldn't help noticing that she made no effort to move away. "It looks like it's TV and Parcheesi. Or something. I'll admit I'm not much of a board game kind of guy."

"Video games?"

"Not really. I bought a console, but shooting pretend people really isn't my thing. I ended up giving it to my nephews." Most people probably would have thought of the whole situation as a waste, but Lucas didn't look at it that way. At least he'd learned that he really wasn't into video games. "I like to read," he went on.

"You do?" she asked, looking surprised.

"Should I be offended that you don't think I'd be the literary type?"

A faint tinge of color flushed the fair skin along her cheekbones. "That's not what I meant. But with the golf and everything—"

"I like golf. It relaxes me."

"You don't seem like someone in much need of relaxation."

Her voice had the faintest teasing note, so Lucas couldn't take offense. Anyway, he knew he had a reputation for being laid-back and easygoing to a fault. Nothing ruffled Lucas Wilcox. Or that's what his family and friends thought. It wasn't necessarily true, though. He was just better at hiding it than some people.

"Depends on the day," he told her. "Anyway, there are members of my clan who work pretty hard at their magic, practicing and so on, but that's not how my talent works. The best thing is to just let it…be."

"That sounds…relaxing."

Beneath her light tone, he thought he heard a touch of envy. "Do you have to practice with yours much?"

She hesitated. "Well, if it's an illusion I've never cast before, I want to try it in advance, just so I know it will be effective." Again a pause, as if she was weighing how much she should tell him. "I have a lot of little illusions set up all over Jerome—harmless things, really, more there to keep the tourists safe and out of our business than anything else. But since they have to trick outsiders on a daily basis, they have to be perfect. So I do practice first, to be safe."

"Can I see one?" Her gift fascinated him. Yes, Connor could change his appearance, but no one else in his clan seemed to have Margot's gift of illusions. He wanted to see it in action.

At first she didn't reply, and he wondered if he'd offended her somehow. Was it not considered kosher amongst the McAllisters to ask for displays of one another's powers?

"Okay," she said at last. "How about this?"

In the next instant, the wall where the TV was embedded above the fireplace turned blank and white, and heavy crimson velvet curtains hung on either side, framing what Lucas realized was a miniature movie screen, sized to fit the space perfectly. An image flickered on that screen, and he saw it was the same weather forecast they'd just been watching, only at a size that dwarfed the sixty-inch screen of his television.

It all looked so real that Lucas wanted to get up so he could run his fingers over the nap of the velvet curtains. "That's…amazing."

"Thank you," she replied calmly. Whatever it took for her to cast that illusion, it didn't seem to be requiring too much of her energy.

"How long will it last?"

"Until I stop it. That is, if I wanted the illusion to stay in place permanently, like the ones back in Jerome, I'd need to refresh it about once a week, because it would start to fade after a while. But otherwise it's basically set it and forget it."

It was a display that staggered him a little. That is, he'd known Margot had to be a very strong witch in order to be tapped as an elder, but this was the first time he'd really seen her powers in action. "Well," he said, attempting to sound casual, "color me impressed. Are both your parents strong witches, too?"

At the question, she stiffened a little. "My mother has a knack with plants. If it's green, she can make it grow. She's a big hit with our neighbors."

Lucas sent her a questioning look, and she smiled, albeit rather unwillingly.

"They grow a lot of pot."

He felt his eyebrows lift even further.

"Pot's kind of a thing in Jerome," she explained. "I mean, it's not as if *everyone* partakes, as it were, but it's definitely part of the culture."

Well, that would explain the slightly off nature of some of the smoke he'd smelled outside the Halloween dance....

"Anyway," she went on, "I'm not sure why my power turned out to be so strong. My father was a civilian."

"Was?" Lucas asked delicately, not sure of what else to say.

"Is," she clarified. "That is, he's still alive. I've just never met him."

Since he couldn't think of a remotely intelligent way to respond to that, Lucas remained silent, waiting to see if she would say anything else, or whether she'd clam up once again.

Then she seemed to give the smallest of sighs. "Oh, I suppose it doesn't make much of a difference one way or another." A small silence, as if she were gathering her thoughts, and then she went on, "My mother wanted a child, but she really didn't want to get married. Didn't want to be tied down, although I have a hard time figuring out what she thought she'd do with a child if she wanted to continue with her free and easy life. Anyway, my father was—is—an Italian artist. He was traveling through the Southwest one summer, painting as he went, and then he came to Jerome and met my mother. They had quite the fling, I guess, and in September his visa was up, and back to Italy he went."

Lucas nodded but didn't reply immediately. Well, Margot's story explained the "Paolo Cantu" in the "Father" section on her birth certificate...and it also explained her dark, lithe looks, which made her stand out amongst the McAllisters, most of whom had hair in shades of light brown and red and even blonde. "Does he...does he know about you?"

"Oh, yes. My mother made it very clear to him that she didn't expect him to support me or anything, but every year for my birthday he'd send me these beautiful little hand-painted cards with Italian scenes on them. Sort of like limited-edition postcards, I guess. He got married a few years after I was born, and I have a grand total of five half-siblings, and a bunch of nieces and nephews." A faint smile. "So I suppose you and I have that in common. I've never met any of them, though, as they've never come to the United States, and obviously I'm a little limited in my ability to travel."

A silence fell. Lucas wasn't sure what he should say...or even if she wanted him to say anything at all. He had a feeling that she'd never told anyone else that story, although of course the members of her clan of her mother's generation would know something of it. At last he cleared his throat and said, "Thank you."

She didn't ask him for what. "You're welcome."

In that moment, the illusion of the weathercast disappeared, and the television went back to normal. The forecaster was saying, "Low pressure is deepening over the four corners region, bringing with it increased chances of snow in northern Arizona and western New Mexico. Up to ten inches of fresh snow are forecast for Flagstaff. A travel advisory has been issued—"

Lucas picked up the remote and shut off the TV. He didn't need to hear any more. Come what may, it looked like his wish to be snowbound here with Margot was about to come true.

Oddly, after she'd unburdened herself of one of her deepest, darkest secrets, Margot felt better about being with Lucas, rather than worse. He'd listened calmly, even sympathetically, and she supposed that he, in his own way, had had as unconventional a childhood as she. It was something else that, against all odds, they had in common.

After that they'd gone back out to the living room, which afforded a much better view of the falling snow. She was glad that Lucas had apparently bought out the local grocery store, since it looked as if the roads were going to be impassable for a good while.

And shouldn't she be a little more upset by that scenario than she was? Even a day earlier, the thought of being trapped in this house with the Wilcox warlock had been enough to bring on mild symptoms of panic. Now, though, she thought she might not mind all that much. She wasn't sure she wanted to analyze what had brought on that particular shift in her attitude.

He got another fire going, and they settled on the couch—not too close to one another—and talked about their families, about what this integration of the clans Angela was urging would mean in the end. In a way, Margot thought it would be easier on the Wilcoxes than the McAllisters. They'd always been the more powerful family, and had never really looked on the Jerome contingent as much of a threat, whereas the McAllisters had a long history of mistrust and fear when it came to the Flagstaff clan.

And the whole time the snow fell, drifting this way and that, deepening and darkening until Lucas had to get up and turn on a few lights.

"Does it get like this often?" she asked, once he'd settled himself back next to her on the couch.

"Define 'often,'" he replied, the corners of his eyes crinkling with amusement. "It's early for a storm this big, but we've had worse as early as October. It's not like Minnesota or something, though—we'll probably wake up tomorrow to blue skies. We don't go weeks and weeks with unending snow or any-thing like that."

The "wake up" comment made her startle a lit-tle, but she realized he wasn't trying to hint at any-thing, was only pointing out that these things rarely lasted all through the day and the night. She squinted out the window, hoping he was right. At the rate that snow was falling, they'd have a hard time opening the back door…not that she really wanted to go out in the weather to test that particular hypothesis.

He glanced at his watch. "Ready for lunch? Actually, let me rephrase—are you ready to make lunch? I'm not sure how much use I'll be."

"Grilled cheese and soup?"

"Sounds perfect." A grimace, and he said, "I am sorry about this. I really intended to take you around town and do the usual wining and dining and so on. I didn't mean to lure you up here just so you could spend the whole time fixing me food."

He looked so rueful that she had to laugh. "It's all right. You wined and dined me just fine last night. I don't mind returning the favor."

And really, she didn't. It was a joy to work in that kitchen, which had three times the counter space she was used to. Lucas did help, too, slicing the cheese for her, then setting the table in the dining room. It was easy enough to whip up a couple of sandwiches and heat up the carton of organic tomato soup she found in the pantry.

Perfect comfort food for a day when they could stay inside, feel sheltered and safe and warm as the snow continued to drift down outdoors. As she ate, Margot thought briefly of her phone, still sitting on the dresser up in the guest bedroom. Perhaps there was a chance that someone had tried to get in touch with her during the last few hours, but she somehow doubted that. Anyway, all anyone back in Jerome had to do was look at the weather reports and realize that Margot Emory wasn't going anyplace anytime soon.

After lunch was eaten and the kitchen cleaned up, Lucas actually did suggest checkers as a way to pass the time. That was fine with her. At least he hadn't tried to get her to play chess. That was a skill she'd never acquired, although it was fun sometimes to watch Boyd and Bryce have one of their grudge matches. They both seemed to take what was only a game so very personally.

But she'd never been all that competitive, so it was easy enough to sit with Lucas in the living room and play game after game, chatting casually about what they might do tomorrow if the weather managed to clear up, and how long it would take to get the roads plowed all over again. The dark outside shifted to the true dark of early evening, and Lucas excused himself for a moment, coming back to the living room with a bottle of wine and two glasses.

"It's after five, so it's safe," he teased.

Margot wasn't sure how safe it really was, actually, but she didn't protest. At the moment, she was feeling warm and relaxed, safe in a way she wasn't sure she'd ever been. Somewhere in the back of her mind, she had the stray thought, *I think I'm okay with this.*

Whatever "this" might be.

Lucas poured some wine into one of the glasses and handed it to her. She held it, waiting until he was done getting some for himself. Afterward, he lifted his glass and said, "Here's to a good ski season."

"Do you ski?" she asked, amused.

"No. One of my cousins broke his leg in two places when we were both in high school, and although our healer patched him up, that sort of cured me of wanting to tackle the slopes. But hey— it's good for the local economy, and someone might as well get some use out of all this snow."

"I'll drink to that."

They clinked glasses, and Lucas and Margot both took a swallow of wine. Yes, that tasted good, and felt even better going down. Rich and fruity, with just the slightest hint of oak. It went well with the fire, with the falling night outside the enormous windows that made up one wall of the room. And yet she didn't feel exposed at all, sitting here like this in their little oasis of light and warmth. Only trees faced the house; the neighbors' homes were safely hidden on either side. So different from Jerome, where you tended to be piled up on one another.

"Are there any other Wilcoxes in this neighborhood?" she asked.

"A couple. My cousin Roxanne and her husband are two streets over, and down on the other side of the hill is my cousin Tom and his family." He shot her a curious look. "Why?"

"Just wondering. It seems like you have so much land to spread out on here, and yet I didn't get to see even a tenth of the town yesterday."

"Sorry about that—"

She waved a hand. "I didn't mean it that way. The weather isn't your fault. It's just nice that you can have your family near…but not *too* near, if you know what I mean."

"It is good to have some privacy," he agreed. Then he paused, his eyes meeting hers, as if to say, *And I know exactly what I'd like to do with that privacy….*

This time the heat that went over her wasn't unwelcome at all…and had nothing to do with the fire in front of her. She drew in a breath, watching Lucas as well, the silence between them growing and growing until it felt almost like a live thing, like some entity their unspoken attraction had given life to.

She didn't know which of them set their glass
down first. All she did know was that suddenly his
fingers were tangling in hers, and he was pulling
her toward him, and then his mouth was on hers,
insistent, as if he'd been holding off for as long as
he could but didn't have the will to do so any longer.
And that was fine, because her resistance seemed to
have fled, leaving nothing but the desire for him, the
need to touch him and taste him, to open her mouth
to his, feel his hands let go of hers and now move to
her shoulders, pulling her close.

Her body pressed against his, and she once again
marveled at how firm and strong he felt, how very
real, as if everything else around her was a dream and
Lucas the only solid thing in it. One hand tangled in
her loose hair, moving up to run over her scalp, and
she shivered at the strangely intimate touch.

He lifted his mouth from hers, whispered
hoarsely, "I want to take you upstairs."

She knew what that meant, also knew that he
was asking her permission, that even now, when she
could feel how aroused he was, he was trying to hold
back, to allow her to retain control of the situation.
Only she didn't want to be in control. She wanted to
let go of everything, every worry, every doubt, every
fear, and revel in the moment, of being with Lucas.

"I want you to take me," she replied, her own
voice barely above a murmur.

That seemed to be enough for him, as he scooped her up in his arms and began to move toward the staircase. Wait—was he actually going to carry her up to his bedroom?

It seemed he was. And she wouldn't protest, would only allow herself to revel in the sensation of being held in his arms like this, of being carried as if she weighed nothing, up all those steps, moving down the upstairs corridor, all the way to his bedroom. At last he yanked back the bedclothes and then set her down, pausing for a second to retrieve something from the nightstand. Margot wasn't sure at first what he was doing, until she realized he'd picked up a remote for the gas fireplace on the opposite side of the room so he could switch it on.

How decadent. She smiled up at him as the fire came to life, seeming to echo the heat rippling along every vein, every nerve ending. His gaze met hers, dark with lust, urgent with need.

"I'm glad you never put your shoes back on," he said, reaching for the button on her jeans and undoing it, then sliding them off.

She gasped, although she wasn't sure if it was the shock of the cool air in the room on her now-exposed flesh, or that he'd moved so quickly, now that he was certain she wanted the same thing he did. To show she was just as much a participant as he, she undid his jeans as well, pulling them down, trying to keep her eyes from widening at the obvious erection straining his gray boxer-briefs. His legs were sturdy, thick with muscle, and she swallowed.

But she didn't have time to dwell on that, because now he was grasping her sweater and the camisole she wore beneath it, and pulling both over her head in one smooth motion. She had the absent thought that he seemed to be fairly expert at removing a woman's clothing, but she decided it was probably best not to dwell on that. Better to be glad that she'd worn her black lace bra and matching bikini, and not something far more matronly. She actually did love pretty lingerie, although she didn't want to examine the impulse that had led her to pack the newer and nicer items for this trip to Flagstaff.

Lucas stood over her, staring down as if he wasn't sure what he should say. Finally he breathed, "You're beautiful, Margot."

She began to shake her head, and he cut in,

"You are. You're perfect."

Fine, she wouldn't protest, but she would cover up her embarrassment by sitting up and unbuttoning his shirt, pulling it off and flinging it to one side. Goddess, but he was beautiful, too, with his broad shoulders and flat stomach, and the heavy muscles of his arms and chest. A fine sprinkling of dark hair there, too, just enough to make her want to run her hands over it. She'd never liked men whose bodies were as smooth as a pre-pubescent boy's.

Once again their gazes locked, and it seemed he could see the admiration in her eyes, because he sank down on the bed next to her, pulling her close, her breasts crushed against his bare chest, his mouth seeking hers once more. One of his hands roamed up her back, found the hooks of her bra, and undid them. It loosened, and he lifted it away from her body, throwing it to join the pile of their other discarded clothing.

Then it was only flesh to flesh as he kissed her again, and her entire body throbbed with need for him, for him to provide the release she'd been wanting for so long, before she would even acknowledge its existence. His thumb hooked into the waistband of her panties, pulling them down, and then his finger was slipping into her, stroking her, and she cried out, pressing against him, fingers digging into his back as he continued to caress her, touching her exactly the way she needed to be touched.

The orgasm slammed through her, causing her not so much to cry out as to actually scream, as if she were giving voice to all the years of pent-up need, releasing those barren days and nights, proclaiming to the world that she actually was still alive. She clung to Lucas, breathing so heavily those breaths might as well have been sobs.

"Hey," his voice came at her ear, a soothing murmur. "Are you all right?"

"I'm fine," she said. "I just—that was incredible."

"You think that was incredible?" he asked, and his voice held the tinge of laughter she knew all too well. "You haven't seen anything yet."

And then he was kissing his way down her stomach, moving lower, and she knew what he was about to do, felt as if she should protest, tell him it was too soon for that...but she wanted it. She wanted his tongue there, wanted him to make her come again.

He moved in slow, luxurious strokes, as if savoring her taste. Her fingers buried themselves in his hair, feeling the life in those thick strands, body pulsing with heat as he made love to her with his tongue. She could feel it building in her, a throbbing need, her very fingers and toes tingling, and then it went off within her, flooding every inch of her body with heat, with rolling waves of ecstasy.

At some point he must have pulled away, but she couldn't have said for sure when, as she could only lie there, limbs trembling, breasts rising and falling as she attempted to draw in breath. Had it ever felt like that before? She didn't think so.

No, she knew it hadn't.

Lucas settled himself down next to her, reaching out to push her hair away from her face. "I've been wanting to do that for a while."

Words seemed to have abandoned her for the moment. She could only roll toward him, reach out and take him in her hand, his shaft so thick and hard she had a hard time getting her fingers to wrap all the way around him. It didn't seem fair that she should be so satisfied, when it was clear he needed his own release. She began to work her hand up and down, and he let out a gasp, his head lolling back against the pillows. His skin under her fingers felt so soft, silk and velvet combined, and it wasn't enough then to simply be touching him. She wanted to taste him, as he'd tasted her, and she bent and took him into her mouth, salt and a faint, faint musk touching her tongue.

Now he groaned, and she continued to suckle him, one hand moving up and down while her tongue worked away at his tip, and she could feel him growing even thicker and harder, if that were possible, his breath going in and out in sharp gasps. Then his hand touched her hair, and he told her in strangled tones, "Stop, Margot. That's incredible, but—I want to be in you. Okay?"

Was that okay? Of course it was. She wanted to be joined with him, hadn't really intended to bring him to climax with her mouth—it was only that she'd gotten a little carried away. "I want that, too," she whispered.

He ran a hand down her hair and over her cheek, a gesture so tender, so gentle, that something in her wanted to weep at his touch. But she didn't, instead maneuvered herself up against the pillows as he reached over and opened the nightstand drawer. She knew what he was doing, wanted to protest, to say that she knew how to protect herself with Brigid's charm—but she didn't. He certainly hadn't lived a celibate life, and although she was sure he'd always taken precautions, it was probably best to be safe now.

A crinkle of the foil packet, and then he was rolling the condom on, his fingers shaking a little. Funny, since she was sure he'd done that hundreds of times before.

But never with me, she thought then, and there was something oddly triumphant in that realization, that she had such an effect on him.

But then she didn't have time to think about anything else, because he was above her, dark eyes intent on hers, his hands planted firmly on either side of her. "Are you ready?" he asked quietly.

Oh, yes, she was ready. Or at least her body was, and she'd worry about her brain later. In this moment, all she wanted was this final connection with him, this consummation that had been desired for far longer than she'd wanted to admit.

"Yes," she replied. "Please, Lucas."

That was all he needed. She was so ready for him that he slipped in easily, despite his girth, and she let out a gasp, then wrapped her legs around him, driving him deeper, wanting him there, in the very core of her being, in that place which had been empty for so long.

He moved slowly at first, then began to slam into her harder and harder, his breath coming in gusts, his jaw tight. Was he trying to hold off, so she might climax first? She didn't know for sure. All she did know was that her limited experience had never prepared her for this, for the sensation that every stroke, every thrust seemed to build in her, her body clenching around him, driving him deeper, her own breathing shallow and trembling.

Goddess help me, I do love this man.

Margot did climax before him, but only by a few seconds. Then she could feel his body tense, and he cried out, slamming into her as the orgasm shuddered its way through his body. He finally collapsed on top of her, but she didn't mind, loved how she could feel his weight pressed against her breasts and her stomach, her legs and her arms. It was as if he wanted to continue the connection, make sure it was felt along every inch of both their bodies.

Eventually, though, he pulled away and more or less collapsed on one side of her. His hand reached out and sought hers, fingers twining around one another, then giving a gentle squeeze. For a long moment, he didn't say anything, seemed content to lie there next to her, their breathing eventually settling and calming. She was glad of the time he was giving her, time she desperately needed to sort out what had just happened. Lucas had made love to her. She couldn't call it just sex. She'd had casual sex before, and this was nothing like that.

Everything had changed, and she didn't know what in the world to do about it.

CHAPTER ELEVEN

LUCAS SENSED MARGOT WASN'T QUITE UP FOR TALKING, so after a long moment he gently released her hand from his, then got up from the bed so he could go to the bathroom and get himself more or less cleaned up. After disposing of the condom and rinsing himself off, he splashed some more water on his face, hoping that would clear his head.

He'd somehow known it would be spectacular, but he still hadn't expected…that. Funny how it was the cool and collected ones who turned out to be the fieriest in bed. Just the merest recollection of the way she had felt, the way she had tasted, made him begin to harden again. Damn. Not that he wouldn't mind going for round two, but he had a feeling Margot might need a little more space than that.

To distract himself, he got a clean pair of under-wear out of the lowboy he kept in the dressing area of his bathroom, then pulled on a fresh T-shirt as well. Hoping that was enough to prove to Margot he wasn't ready to start all over again, he went back out to the bedroom. She had already put her underwear back on, and was just picking up her camisole from where it had landed on the floor.

"Hungry?" he asked, and she started.

"What?"

"Well, it's almost seven. I was wondering if you were hungry."

Seeming to consider, she paused, camisole still in one hand. Lucas was just fine if she wanted to stay like that, so he could enjoy looking at the curve of her breasts as defined by the black lace bra she wore. Who knew she'd be hiding something that hot under the simple clothing she wore?

Then she said, "I do think I worked up some-thing of an appetite."

Something about the small smile that played around her mouth as she gave him that reply made a wave of heat pass over him. To hide his obvious reaction, he bent and picked up his jeans from the floor, and hoped he'd be able to get them on over his growing erection.

"Well, let's see what we can rustle up," he

replied, repressing a groan as he stuffed himself into his pants.

She nodded and slipped into her own jeans, then pulled her sweater over her head. As she did so, he grabbed his discarded shirt and drew it on, fingers fumbling with the buttons. Amazing how he was still feeling tremors from that orgasm.

Or maybe not so amazing. He'd been with a lot of women, but never one like Margot.

If she noticed the effect she'd had on him, she showed no sign of it. After pulling on her socks, she waited for him as he finished the last of his buttons, then headed for the door.

"Aren't you going to turn that off?" she inquired, inclining her head toward the fireplace.

"No," he said. "It'll help to keep the room warm. A night like this, with all that snow piled up on the roof? The furnace can use all the help it can get. I figured you'd rather come back to a warm bed." And then he stopped himself, because he realized he'd made a pretty big assumption there. Just because they'd slept together, it didn't mean they would actually…sleep together.

But she didn't contradict him, only said, "Yes, I would."

Again he could feel himself flush with heat, needing her all over again, but she'd basically just made him a promise that this wasn't going to be a one-time occurrence.

He really couldn't ask for much more than that.

It should have been awkward to bustle around the kitchen, rustling up dinner after the experience they'd just shared, but strangely, it wasn't. Again Margot found herself enjoying the process, getting out the chicken breasts, simmering them with the sauce Lucas had bought. Maybe Rachel McAllister would have tisk-tisked at using something pre-made like that, but Margot had to admit that it did really speed up the process.

Lucas brought the mostly empty bottle of wine in from the living room, and they finished it off while she cooked, finding herself lightheaded, but not really tipsy. No, it wasn't the wine that made her feel giddy. It was Lucas Wilcox.

She knew she shouldn't be feeling this way. Bad enough that they'd had sex, but sex was something you could walk away from, no strings attached. But this warmth in her breast every time she looked at him, the way her breath wanted to catch when he turned around and those dark eyes, a warm brown that contrasted with the near-black of his hair, caught hers? Bad news. Very bad news. It meant she cared. Cared a lot. She'd already whispered the "L" word in her mind, but now she found it even more difficult to acknowledge. She loved him, and she'd slept with him.

Some people might say she'd gone way, way past the point of no return.

He came up behind her, pushed her hair away from the back of her neck. The warmth of his lips touched the sensitive skin, and her body heated with need all over again.

"That smells good," he said, once he'd straightened up again.

She wasn't sure if he meant her skin or her hair or the food she was cooking. Maybe it didn't really matter. "It should be ready soon."

"Then I'd better get the table set."

Her gaze followed him as he went out to the dining room, his hands full with cutlery and paper napkins. The place mats they'd used for lunch were still sitting on the table, so it didn't take much time for him to get set up. But she liked watching him go to and fro, watching the way he moved, the strength of his body under the casual loose-fitting clothing. She realized then that he was dressed very much like he'd been in that one photo with his mother, where he'd been barely more than a boy.

He was definitely all man now, though. More man than she'd ever thought she'd have.

Somehow she managed to will away the throbbing that particular thought brought on, and focused on getting the food transferred to dishes and bowls. It was all pretty easy—the chicken in the mole sauce, the rice, the black beans. And when she began to bring it out, she noticed that Lucas had opened another bottle of wine.

She lifted an eyebrow at him, and he grinned. "Were you planning on driving anywhere?"

No, she wasn't. The only place she planned to go at the end of the evening was right back into his bed. Maybe sooner. "Not really. It just feels...decadent."

"I think it's time you let your hair down, don't you?"

Oh, yes. Loose and wild and free, just the way she was feeling now. Reality would probably catch up eventually, but in the meantime she planned to enjoy herself.

They sat down, and Lucas poured her some wine while she settled her napkin in her lap. When he raised his glass, he said, "What should we toast?"

Her gaze strayed to the high windows in the living room, where snow was still falling, pale blurs against the black of night. Goddess bless the snow, the cocoon of privacy and isolation it provided. She lifted her glass as well. "To snowstorms."

"To snowstorms," he echoed, clinking his wine glass against hers.

They drank. It was a tempranillo this time, a good pairing with the chicken mole, which turned out to be surprisingly tasty, considering the sauce had come out of a pouch. And although Margot had expected some awkwardness, there really wasn't any. They talked some more about their families, about how Lucas had a degree from Northern Pines in mathematics, of all things. That surprised her more than she cared to admit, but he only shrugged and said, "I always liked numbers. It was something Damon and I enjoyed talking about. There's something pure about math. And it's helped a lot with financial planning for the clan."

He was so off-hand about the whole thing that she let it go, and made herself still her own tiny pang of jealousy. Not that she would have lasted two months as a math major, but just that he had the opportunity to stay in his clan's territory and still go to a real four-year university, where the only thing Cottonwood had to offer was a community college. True, there was Embry-Riddle over in Prescott, although it had never been an option for her, as she wasn't interested in aviation or engineering. That had been Clay's field of expertise.

She shut that thought down right away. Here, enjoying the afterglow of the lovemaking with Lucas and listening to the warm timbre of his voice, admiring the way the candlelight lent an additional warmth to his olive-toned skin, the last thing she wanted to think about was Clay McAllister.

And from time to time she would pause in the conversation and notice the way Lucas was watching her, like a child who couldn't really believe that his parents had gotten him a pony for Christmas, but even that didn't feel awkward. More…empowering, that she should be on the receiving end of such admiration and astonishment.

Then the lights flickered and went out, and Margot gave a little gasp. They weren't in complete darkness, as the tapers on the table had been lit, and a faint glow emanated from the living room, where the fire still burned.

"Does this happen often?" she asked. It certainly did back in Jerome, where during a good thunderstorm her cottage stood about a fifty-fifty chance of losing power, but she'd thought things would be more robust here, as they were so much newer.

He shrugged, looking supremely unconcerned. "From time to time. It's not that big a deal. It'll come on eventually. And the heat is gas, and so are the water heater and the stove, so we don't really have that much to worry about."

No, they didn't. They had the fire, and candlelight, and each other. She drank some more wine, then said, "So I suppose that rules out watching anything on that big flat-screen of yours."

His teeth flashed as he smiled. "No, I had something a little better in mind."

Thank God the fireplace in his bedroom was natural gas as well. It lent warmth and a dim, intimate light to the room, making Margot appear like some goddess of flame and shadow in its reflection as she laughed and set her glass of wine down on the nightstand, then pulled her sweater over her head. She did so with almost a forced boldness, as if she'd never done something like that before, had always waited for her partner to undress her.

He was hard already, watching her. No, scratch that—he'd been hard during almost the whole dinner, listening to the soft, low tones of her voice, seeing that tumble of dark hair fall free on her shoulders. He'd done his best to ignore his body's response to her, but now that he was here with her again in his bedroom, he didn't have to deny any longer what she did to him.

Following her lead, he drew off his own clothes, fingers clumsy in their hastiness to get rid of the annoying pieces of cloth that stood between him and feeling her satiny skin against his once more. She pulled back the covers and climbed into his bed, then waited for him there, naked, skin so pale and perfect against the warm brown of the sheets.

In reality it was probably only about thirty seconds, but it felt like an eternity before he could be there in bed next to her, his body pressed against her, the exquisite softness of her breasts rubbing against his chest. He ran his hands over her, wanting to touch every part of her, sliding down her slender waist, over the curve of her hips, down to where she was so wet and ready for him.

Her eyes shut, lashes dark and full against the pallor of her skin, and her breathing quickened, breasts rising and falling as she gasped and writhed against him. So, so responsive. Her passion still surprised him, but he wasn't going to question it, wasn't going to do anything except touch her, fingers gliding over her, stroking her, until he felt her spasm around him, shudders moving through her entire body.

She reached out to touch him then, and he groaned as her fingers wrapped around him, working slowly, deliberately, not too fast or too hard—he could tell she wanted him to last as long as possible. That wouldn't be easy, not with the way he'd been aroused for the better part of an hour already. But he slowed his breathing to work in concert with her caresses, knowing he didn't want to spend himself in her hand.

And then she let go of him, shifted, began to move so she would be on top of him. Somehow he summoned the strength to take her by the arms, to hold her in place and say, "Wait—I have to get a condom—"

"No," she cut in. "I want to feel you. *Really* feel you. Promise me it'll be safe."

"It will," he gasped. "I've got stock in Trojan. But you—"

"I'll use the charm to protect me."

"Because that worked so well for Angela."

Her expression grew severe—or as severe as it could, given that her lips were still parted, swollen with his kisses, her eyes wide, dark pools of desire. "Extenuating circumstances. You're not the next *primus*, Lucas—there's no supernatural biological imperative to deal with here."

"Oh, there's a biological imperative," he began, but he didn't get any further than that, as she lowered herself onto him, and he felt her warmth surround him. Her eyes closed, and she let out a moan, and that was the end of any self-control he might have possessed. He began to move with her, plunging deeper and deeper into her as she rocked her hips in time with his thrusts. Had there ever been anything as beautiful as her riding him, head tilted back, long dark hair falling to brush against his thighs? Her hands crept up to cup her breasts, and he'd thought he was aroused before, but now, seeing her caress herself like that, completely lost in the moment, he couldn't hold himself back, burying himself in her, knowing he wouldn't be able to hold on much longer.

Like a late summer cloudburst, the orgasm swept over him, wrenching a moan from his throat and an answering cry from Margot. Her eyes were still shut, and then he could feel her clenching around him, feel her own climax hit, and they both rode the aftershocks for a few seconds afterward, until at last she collapsed onto the bed next to him, gasping, her body shuddering. She lay there for a little while, and then let out a little hiccuping laugh and said, "I think I need to get cleaned up."

The downside of not using a condom. He lay there, too spent to move, as she somehow managed to wriggle out of bed and totter into the bathroom. The water ran for a bit, and then she returned and picked up her underwear. After a pause, she shook her head. "I think I need to duck into my room and get some clean things."

He nodded. "I'm not going anywhere."

She flashed him a quick smile, retrieved the rest of her clothes, and hurried out into the corridor. While she was gone, he might have dozed a bit; he couldn't be sure how long it had been, but now she was wearing a dark red sleep shirt of some kind, and her face looked glossy and clean. Under other circumstances, he might have minded the shirt, but in a way it was sexy, as it revealed her long, slim legs and was low-cut enough to show the faintest hint of the shadow between her breasts, and yet covered everything else up.

When she slid in next to him and kissed him, he tasted the mint on her breath and realized she must have brushed her teeth. "You still had some wine left," he pointed out.

"It's all right. I really didn't want any more."

That seemed to be the signal they were done for the night, which meant he should probably get moving and brush his teeth as well. It took him a minute to summon the energy, but eventually he got up, splashed some water on his face, and then climbed back in the bed. His eyes didn't immediately adjust to the fire-lit darkness of his bedroom after the bright illumination in the bathroom, but when they did, he saw that Margot was lying on her back, staring up at the ceiling.

"Hey," he said. "What're you thinking about?"

She hesitated for so long that he wasn't certain she planned to reply. "Just…thinking."

He could practically feel the turmoil within her, now that some of the effects of their lovemaking had subsided. The situation didn't have to be this difficult for her, but it seemed as if she was determined to make it so, as if she couldn't accept that the two of them were meant to be together. Well, time to make her realize she didn't have any choice but to accept it.

"Okay, here's a question," he said. "But I want you to promise me one thing."

Rolling over so she could face him, she replied, "Promise you what?"

"That when I ask you this question, you'll answer quickly. Don't think. Feel. Tell me from your gut."

She gave a not very convincing laugh. "That sounds ominous."

"Just promise."

"Okay, I promise."

He drew in a breath. "If someone asked you what you wanted, what you *really* wanted, for your life…what would you tell them?"

Although she'd promised, he'd still expected her to stop, weigh it in her mind, and then tell him something she thought was correct but wasn't actually what she truly wanted.

But she stared straight at him, eyes dark and unblinking. "I'd tell them that I wanted to be with you, here, in this house. With no one else…and in no place else."

Something hot and heavy seemed to grow in his chest, and he reached out and pulled her against him, kissing the crown of her head, holding her so close he could feel the beating of her heart within her breast. "Then we'll just have to figure out a way to make that happen."

CHAPTER TWELVE

THIS MORNING WHEN MARGOT AWOKE, SHE KNEW EXACTLY where she was: nestled in Lucas' bed, curled up next to him, the warmth of his body combining with the weight of the blankets and comforter on top of them to make her deliciously cozy. The light peeking around the blinds was pale gray, not the brooding bruised color of a truly stormy sky. And blinking on the nightstand next to her was his clock/iPod dock, proving that the power must have come back on sometime during the night.

She wasn't sure if she wanted to move. Truth be told, she didn't know what she should do. Last night, still half tipsy—and still drunk with the afterglow of another round of spectacular sex—she'd told him she wanted to be with him here. What had possessed her? Yes, it had been the deepest truth of her heart, but even though he'd assured her they would figure out a way to make it work, she didn't share his optimism. Coming up for a three-day snowbound fling was one thing. Moving past that to contemplate a life together? Not quite so simple, was it?

Beside her, Lucas stirred, and she felt him reach beneath the covers to touch her fingers, give them a squeeze. His eyes seemed to focus on her, and he said, "Sweetheart, it's way too early to be looking that worried."

"Sorry."

"No need to apologize. It's just that, even though it might feel that way, the weight of the world really isn't on your shoulders."

Easy for him to say. Yes, he was definitely someone Connor confided in, but Lucas held no formal role in his clan, didn't have the pressure of generations of tradition bearing down on him.

"Maybe you're right," she said reluctantly, more because she didn't want to quarrel with him first thing than because she believed what she was saying. "I think I just need a shower."

"Can I join you?" he asked, eyes glinting.

There was an idea. But she'd already allowed sex to distract her more than she should, and she knew exactly what would happen if she got into a shower with Lucas Wilcox. "How about next time?"

Thank the Goddess, he didn't look all that disappointed. "I'll definitely take a rain check on that one."

Because all her toiletries and fresh clothes were still in the guest bedroom, she went there to shower. Any hoped-for illumination didn't materialize between the shampoo and conditioner, and when she got out to towel off, she was just as conflicted as when she'd begun.

As if hoping that a text or voicemail would be the sign from the gods she needed, she went over to the dresser and inspected her phone. It still had a full charge, so the power must not have been out all that long. The phone was also completely devoid of any contact from her fellow elders, or from anyone at all, for that matter. She wished she could blame the communications blackout on connection issues caused by the storm, but she had four out of five bars here, meaning that anything someone sent her should have gotten through easily.

Obviously, I'm not as important as I think I am.

Feeling annoyed, and then annoyed with herself for being annoyed, she finished dressing, slipped some silver hoops into her ears, and went back into the hallway. From Lucas' room she could hear the shower running, so she decided to head downstairs and make some tea. Not that she really expected a cup of tea to help much with clearing her head, but at least it gave her something to do.

Today she knew her way around much better, so she got the tea going without much delay, did the same with Lucas' Italian roast and the automatic coffeemaker, and then went to the kitchen door so she could gaze out on what the snow had wrought. All of his hard work of the day before had been more or less erased, the driveway now buried in what had to be more than a foot of snow. She felt a pang of dismay on his behalf, and wished he had two snowblowers so she could at least help him get it cleared.

Speaking of clear, the clouds overhead looked as if they had actually begun to part, patches of blue appearing above the snow-crowned tops of the ponderosa pines. That had to be a good thing, an indication that the storm was moving on.

As she was pouring hot water into a mug, Lucas appeared in the kitchen, scrubbed and smiling, hair damp. "I thought I smelled coffee. Thanks for getting it going."

"It seemed the least I could do."

He bent down and kissed her then, and she breathed in the clean scent of his freshly washed skin and hair. What was it that made a man smell so good? She wasn't sure, but she knew she wanted to wake up to Lucas every day just so she could breathe deeply of his scent.

All right, that wasn't the *only* reason she wanted to wake up next to him every day....

She turned away and watched him pour himself a cup of coffee. Today he was wearing more jeans and a Northern Pines sweatshirt. Had Damon given it to him, or had he bought it himself? She supposed it really didn't matter, but something in her felt a little pang for Lucas and the friendship he'd lost. It had been easy for her to hate Damon; he was merely a figure of fear to her and the others in her clan, not a man at all. Now, though, she realized it had been a little more complicated than that, and she could only wish him peace, wherever he'd ended up.

Lucas wandered over to the door and peered through the thick glass, a resigned look on his face. "Looks like I'll be hitting that driveway again after breakfast."

"But at least it's clearing up."

His features brightened a bit. "True. I think we're out of the woods for now."

Was he talking about more than just the storm? She flickered a quick glance at him, but she couldn't tell anything from the placid, pleasant expression he currently wore.

"Then I suppose I'd better get some breakfast together before you go out and break your back a second time."

He brightened up at her suggestion. "That sounds good."

It was another round of scrambled eggs, this time with sausage and toast. When they sat at the counter to eat, their legs brushed against one another, and Margot felt her body grow warm just at that casual touch. It was enough that she felt like taking him by the hand and pulling him back upstairs. But no, he had things to do, and she needed to learn how to restrain herself. Anyway, if he got all sweaty from clearing off the driveway again and had to take another shower, maybe that would be the time to cash in that rain check....

Snow check, she thought then, and fought back an implausible giggle. Margot Emory did not giggle. And yet...right now, she sort of wanted to. Despite everything.

As they had yesterday, she cleaned up breakfast, and he went to get "suited up" for another round in the driveway. Unlike the day before, however, he gave her a strong, hearty kiss before he went, one tasting of coffee, and she thought she could tolerate coffee when exposed to it that way. A few minutes later, she heard the roar of the snowblower, and hoped the noise wouldn't irritate the neighbors too much. After all, it had to be barely nine in the morning; she didn't know for sure, as all the digital clocks in the kitchen were still blinking. Then she had to remind herself that yes, it was early, but it was also a weekday. Presumably the neighbors to either side were not independently wealthy warlocks, and therefore had to get up and go to work, necessitating an even earlier driveway clearing than the one Lucas was currently engaged in.

Fixing the clocks was something useful she could do for him, so she fetched her phone—still free of texts or voicemails or emails—and used the time on it to reset everything. Well, everything she could reach. There was a clock high up in the living room that would have to be Lucas' problem, but otherwise she took care of things as best she could.

That didn't occupy her for very long, however, so she wandered back to the family room, thinking maybe she'd turn on the weather again to make sure the snow really had gone away for the fore-seeable future. When she entered the room, however, she noticed for the first time the phone sitting on the built-in desk at the back wall, as well as the doodled-over pad of paper next to it. Smiling, she recalled how Lucas had praised her sketch, and said his scribbles were the real doodling.

She'd read somewhere that studying doodles could tell you a lot about a person, but frankly, she couldn't remember which sorts of scribbles and underlines and comic faces were supposed to represent which personality traits. On the pad he'd left behind, there were concentric circles and extremely symmetrical 3-D boxes and triangles, as well as stars in a variety of shapes and sizes. In amongst the scribbles, she saw phone numbers and names, a few she recognized, including Angela's. And then at the bottom, outlined by a large emphatic circle, was the somewhat cryptic message, *Buy Lester lunch sometime to say thanks.*

Who was Lester? Margot didn't recall hearing of any Wilcox clan member with that name, although she had to admit she wasn't familiar with most of them. And what was Lucas grateful for, that he wanted to buy this person lunch?

Knowing Lucas, it could be something as simple as loaning him a box of golf tees, although they were a little past golf season at this point. She shrugged and turned on the TV, hoping it wouldn't take Lucas quite as long this time to clear off the driveway.

He came in through the mudroom on the side of the house and left his snow-encrusted waders there. Time for another shower, probably, and he hoped that maybe he could convince Margot to join him this time. Or, even better, climb into the whirlpool tub and soak away the knots in his shoulders from brute-forcing the snowblower up and down the driveway. He hardly ever used the bathtub, but maybe if they gathered up some candles from elsewhere in the house, ran the hot water, and soaked together before progressing to even more pleasurable activities?

That could definitely work.

From the sound of it, she was in the family room, with the TV on again. He paused in the doorway and admired the sight of her sitting on the couch, attention fixed on the forecast. Her makeup was minimal today, just a bit of mascara and color on her lips, from what he could tell, and he liked her that way. She was so beautiful that she really didn't need much embellishment.

"So are we really in the clear?" he asked.

She turned away from the television, a smile touching her lips. He hoped he could make her smile like that often, because he loved the way it softened her face, brought a glow to those wide, dark eyes.

"Looks that way. At least for the next couple of days. They think there might be another storm coming in late on the weekend."

That didn't bother him, although it was a little unusual to get snow in such rapid succession this early in the year. "Well, I'll worry about that when it hits." He hesitated, then said, "And you? I know you'd talked about going back to Jerome today, but since you hardly got to see anything of Flagstaff—"

"I told the other elders I'd be coming home today." Strangely, though the words themselves were emphatic enough, her tone wasn't, indicating that she was having second thoughts on the subject.

"Any reason why you couldn't stay, other than that?" He tried to keep the urgency out of his voice. Surely she must guess how much he wanted her to remain here for as long as possible, but he also didn't want to sound as if he was pressuring her.

"Not really. I packed an extra change of clothes, just in case." Her smile turned sly. "But if I stay any longer than that, I'm going to run out of underwear."

That's really not what I'd consider a problem, he thought. "We do have a mall here, you know."

"Ah, so now you're tempting me with shopping."

"Don't think of it as tempting...think of it as providing you with useful information."

With a laugh, she reached for the remote, shutting off the TV before getting to her feet. "By the way, who's Lester?"

The sweat on his back seemed to suddenly congeal into ice. "Uh...why do you ask?"

"I saw his name on the pad by the phone. Maybe I was snooping a little." Her gaze was fixed on him, but he didn't see any suspicion there, only a bit of rueful amusement at her poking around the place while he was otherwise occupied.

Not that he could really call it snooping, when he'd been stupid enough to leave the pad sitting out on the desk in plain view of anyone who might pass by. "He's...a friend."

"Oh. One of your golf friends?"

It would be so easy to lie. All he'd have to do was say yes, and then they could go on as if nothing had happened. But he hated lying. His mother's lying to herself and everyone around her had sucked her into a marriage and a family she really didn't want, and Lucas had been forced to deal with the consequences ever since. And what good would his relationship with Margot be if he lied to her from the very beginning?

"No," he said at last. "He's a private investigator."

"Really?" Then her gaze sharpened, as if she'd begun to put two and two together in her head. "What would you need with a private investigator?"

"I—" His mouth was dry, and the words wanted to stick in his throat. Somehow he made himself force them out. "I asked him to find out a thing or two about you. Mostly that you weren't seeing anyone."

The longest, most hideous silence he'd ever heard. She stood there, dark eyes boring into him, as if she'd never seen him before, as if they hadn't just spent the most rapturous night of his entire life together. Finally, "You *what?*"

"Margot, I know it was stupid, but I had no one to ask. It was harmless. Really."

"You think hiring a private investigator to dig up dirt on me is *harmless?*"

"It wasn't digging up dirt. I just needed to know that you were…available." God, the words were coming out of his mouth, but they just kept sounding worse and worse. At least, that was how it felt to him, and if he thought that way, he could only imagine what Margot must be thinking. Her elegant brows were drawn together, her eyes, which had been so filled with laughter a minute ago, now colder than the snow piled up against the house.

"You couldn't ask Angela? You two seem pretty friendly!"

"I thought about it, but she was so busy with the wedding that I decided not to bother her. And there wasn't anyone else I could ask. It's just—I couldn't stop thinking about you, Margot. I tried to tell myself I shouldn't, but it wasn't that easy."

She didn't reply, only continued to stare at him, arms crossed over her breasts. A protective gesture, and one he hated to see.

"Would you rather I had lied to you?" he asked then, his tone hardening.

"No," she said. "I'd rather you'd not done something so stupid in the first place." Her eyes seemed to glitter, and he realized it wasn't from anger, but from unshed tears. She swallowed. "I think I'd better go."

Stepping away from the couch, she headed toward the doorway, and Lucas knew all he had to do was block it, just stand there so she couldn't go anywhere at all, would have to stay and hash this out with him. Something inside told him this would be the very worst thing of all to do, so he stepped out of the way, let her pass him in a waft of soft perfume and cold, cold anger.

And then she was gone.

Somehow she managed to keep it together as she went upstairs and packed her things, then waited in icy silence for Lucas to open the garage door so she could back her car out. Thank the Goddess that he'd cleared the driveway, because otherwise she probably would've stomped out of there on foot if she had to.

What the *hell* had he been thinking? A private investigator? Really?

Once or twice he'd attempted to make an apology, but she'd shut him down with a frigid stare. She didn't want to talk about this. She only wanted to go home, so she could put this entire episode behind her and forget that it had ever happened.

Never mind that until Lucas' startling revelation, she'd been happier than she'd been in…forever. Had Clay ever made her feel remotely that good?

She really didn't want to answer that question.

Although the freeway had been plowed, it was still icy and treacherous enough. In a way, Margot was glad of that. It forced her to concentrate on the road, and not what had just happened between Lucas and her. The Subaru had all-wheel drive, so it wasn't as if she'd had to break out the snow chains or anything, but she still white-knuckled it out of Flagstaff and down past Mountainaire and Munds Park, until at last she dropped to an elevation where there was little evidence of the storm at all, save a few patches of snow here and there in the shadow of a rocky outcropping.

Thinking some music might help fill the throbbing silence that pounded against her ears, she jacked her iPhone into the car stereo and flipped to her favorite '90s mix. That didn't last long, though. A two songs, and then there was Green Day mocking her.

...I hope you had the time of your life....

She gave the phone a vicious swipe to unlock it and jabbed the "pause" button. Quiet filled the car again, and she swallowed, hard. The whole way down I-17, tears threatened to fall, but she wouldn't let them, kept blinking them back. She wouldn't cry. She wouldn't allow Lucas Wilcox to make her cry.

By the time she got off the interstate, she wouldn't say she felt better, exactly, but at least she didn't feel as if she would shatter into a thousand pieces if someone touched her. She drove through Cottonwood and Clarkdale, wound up into Jerome, and then turned into her driveway, just as she had thousands of times before. A touch of the remote, and then she was safely inside her garage, the door shutting behind her, sealing her away from the outside world.

In that moment, it seemed she couldn't bear to look at her luggage, look at the evidence of the time she'd spent with Lucas. Fine. She'd unpack later, once she'd gathered the ragged remains of her composure. Instead, she went in the house, tried to ignore how empty and quiet it seemed, and decided to make some tea, not because she really wanted any, or because she thought it would help, but because she couldn't think of a damn thing else to do.

It did help, actually, a tiny bit. She took her mug of tea and went to sit on the back porch, which looked over the carefully tended yard, the roses dead-headed and awaiting their winter dormancy, the grass already beginning to appear a little yellowed, now that they'd had a couple of good frosts.

A shadow fell over the garden path, and Margot looked up, heart giving an irrational thump. He couldn't have come here to plead with her, could he?

But no, it was only Allegra Moss. Margot might have wondered how her fellow elder could have known she was home already, except that Allegra was one of those people who seemed to know every-thing about everyone, or at least gave a very good imitation of it. Besides, her house was just down on the corner, and so she would've seen Margot's car passing by if she'd been looking out the window at the right moment. Which, since it was Allegra, tended to happen more often than not.

"You're back?" Allegra asked, and Margot tried not to wince.

"Yes," she said shortly, hoping the other woman would hear the finality in her tone and not pry, and also knowing, since it was Allegra, that it was a vain hope at best. "I did say it would be three days at the *very* most. Besides, I didn't want to get caught in any weather, in case more snow moved in."

"That makes sense." The older witch paused for a moment, blue eyes keen. Margot thought they might as well have been equipped with X-rays. "Didn't it go well?"

"I don't want to talk about it," Margot said shortly, fingers tightening around her mug so she wouldn't give in to the urge to hurl it at Allegra's head.

"Oh, that's too bad. He seems like such a nice person. And oh, so easy on the eyes."

"Does your husband know you talk like that about other men?" She really didn't want to think about how easy on the eyes Lucas was, because that would get her thinking about his smile, and the light in his dark eyes as he gazed at her, or the way his body had felt pressed against hers....

Allegra laughed, and that helped dispel those unwelcome memories of just how much Margot had enjoyed being around Lucas, being with him. "My dear, I may be married, but I'm not blind."

There not being much Margot could say in reply to that, she only shrugged and sipped at her tea.

"Well," Allegra said, and now she did look vaguely uncomfortable, as if she just realized she'd intruded on something that really was none of her business, "I'll let you relax and unwind, then. I suppose you'll be making the rounds tomorrow morning, checking the illusions?"

"Don't I always?"

"Yes, you do. You're always so reliable, Margot, and don't think that everyone doesn't appreciate it. Enjoy your day." Off she went, momentary discomfort forgotten. No doubt within the hour she'd have latched onto something else to occupy her attention. It was just Allegra's way, and Margot couldn't even really fault her for that.

Even so, she settled back against the creaky wicker of her seat and let out a long sigh.

Reliable.

It seemed that was all she would ever be. Lucas had given her a glimpse of something else, something more, but she'd been foolish to think it could ever come true for her. No, he'd shown himself to be what she'd always feared…a Wilcox, untrustworthy, plotting, covering his deception with a handsome face.

She really didn't want to stop and think how he'd actually gotten himself in trouble by making the simple mistake of telling her the truth.

CHAPTER THIRTEEN

AFTER THE GARAGE DOOR SHUT AND MARGOT DROVE away, Lucas slowly went back into the house, shoulders drooping. There must have been something he could have done to prevent her from leaving, but damn him if he could think of what it might be.

As he entered the kitchen, his gaze fell on the glazed mug she'd used for her tea, still sitting on the counter next to the sink. He went over and picked it up, pressed his lips against the faint trace of the lipstick she'd left there, as if he could somehow recover some of the warmth of her touch by doing so. But the ceramic was cold and hard under his lips, and he shut his eyes, then growled, "Fuck!" before hurling the mug against the wall and watching it shatter into hundreds of pieces.

"Lucky" Lucas, his ass.

Hands clenched into fists, he left the kitchen and the mess he'd just made, stalking through the house with no particular destination in mind. It didn't seem to matter where he went, though—it was now as if his home had been permanently imprinted with Margot's presence, the ghost trace of her perfume. Margot bent over the checkerboard in the living room, dark hair haloed by firelight. Margot sitting at the dining room table and lifting a glass of blood-colored wine in response to his toast. Margot in his bed, flushed with desire, waiting for him.

How could she have done this when she'd only been here for two and a half days? How had she managed to do such a good job of insinuating herself into his home, into his life?

Into his heart?

Now he was glad for all those empty years, those times when he'd met women, seen them a few times, bedded them...and then forgot them, heart and mind untouched. He'd never done anything to hurt any of them, had always broken things off before they got too serious. All that time he'd wondered what was wrong with him, that all around him people seemed perfectly capable of falling in love and settling down, and yet there he was, alone when the rest of the world appeared to be pairing off. Now, though, he understood there was a price for making a connection. Because if that connection somehow was broken, it hurt worse than anything else ever could.

Eventually, he ended up sitting in the living room, staring out the tall windows at the snow-encrusted pines, the deep, deep snow drifts. At some point the snow would begin to melt, but now the temperature was still low enough that everything seemed in stasis, held in some perfect balancing point between light and dark, cold and warmth.

He glimpsed some motion then, saw a doe pick her way out from between the trees, stop in the middle of the backyard, and lift her head, as if smelling the wind. Her ears flicked this way and that, and it seemed that her dark gaze fastened on him, catching him watching her. Lucas didn't move, barely dared to breathe. He didn't want to frighten her off by making any sudden movements, since he wasn't sure if she could even see him through the window glass.

Then she shook, turning away from him and moving back into the stand of pines. Heading south.

In that moment, he knew what he had to do.

Margot eventually got her suitcases out of the trunk, unpacked everything, putting the clothes she hadn't worn back in the closet, depositing the items that needed laundering in the hamper. It felt right. That way, she was putting a period on her little episode with Lucas Wilcox. A fling, a bout of momentary madness. No one could really blame her for kicking up her heels a bit, as long as nothing changed in the end. To tell the truth, she should probably be grateful to him for showing his true colors, for letting her know he wasn't quite as harmless as he pretended to be. Now she could settle back into her life again. In a few months, she would have forgotten all about him.

As the afternoon wore on, clouds began to gather again. So much for the forecasters saying the next few days would be clear. She switched on a few lamps, and, because the wind had picked up and chilly air was finding its way around the out-of-true door frames and chinks in the windowsills, she set a spark to the fire in the grate. There, all was cozy and quiet, just the way she liked it. In a little while, she'd go fix herself some soup, then settle out here with the book she'd forgotten to take with her up to Flagstaff. Perfect. Everything back to how it should be.

Someone knocked on the door, and she frowned. That had better not be Allegra, returning with some kind of manufactured errand. Margot somehow doubted it, though; it was almost six, and they tended to eat early in the Moss household.

She went to the door and opened it. Lucas stood there, staring down at her.

At first she was so startled she didn't quite know what to do. Then she gathered the rags of her composure and asked coldly, "What do you want?"

"To talk."

"I don't think we have anything to talk about."

The wind picked up in that moment, skirling around the corners of the house. She almost thought she felt a ghostly drop of moisture hit her cheek.

"Actually, we do." He hiked his jacket up around his neck, obviously trying to shield himself somewhat from the biting wind. "And it's starting to rain. You're not going to leave me out here to get soaked, are you?"

She was tempted to. And was this more of his "luck" at work, that he'd show up just as the weather turned nasty again so she'd be compelled to invite him inside?

Even as she contemplated the idea, she knew she wouldn't. Just yesterday she'd thought she loved this man. If she were going to be perfectly honest with herself...although she really didn't want to be...she knew she still loved him. Was blazingly angry with him, yes. But now, looking at him, at the way those dark eyes were fixed on her face, pleading, at the lines of the mouth she'd thought she'd never get enough of, she knew it wasn't as easy to turn love off and on as she thought.

"Come in," she said, attempting to keep her tone as neutral as possible.

Obviously, that hadn't worked as well as she would have liked, because his face lit up as he crossed the threshold, then hesitated in the entry, glance going uncertainly to the coat rack in the corner. No doubt he was wondering if she'd allow him to take off his jacket.

"Oh, go ahead," she snapped. "I'll make some coffee."

"Don't go to any trouble on my account," he told her, and she shot him a pained look.

"It's a little late for that."

He took the hint and went into the living room, while she headed to the kitchen, accompanied by a strong sense of déjà vu. Was the universe somehow conspiring to get her together with Lucas Wilcox? Maybe. But the universe was about to discover it had met its match in Margot Emory.

She got the coffee going and made herself a fresh cup of tea while the coffee percolated. Right then she wished for something a bit stronger than tea, but that wasn't happening. Especially when she could blame wine for some of her loosened inhibitions when it came to the man currently waiting in her living room.

No, don't think about that. Just concentrate on getting the coffee put together.

At least he took it black. That made things somewhat easier. She didn't bother with a tray this time, only doctored her tea in the kitchen, then picked up his mug in her left hand and the tea in her right, and went back out to meet him.

"Here," she said, not caring how ungracious she sounded.

He took the mug from her. "Thanks."

She wouldn't bother to say that he was welcome. He wasn't welcome, not here in her house, not in her life. There wasn't anything he could say to her that would make her change her mind.

Seeming to sense her mood, he blew on the coffee but didn't look at her. As he stared at the fire, he said, "I know I screwed up. But when Lester offered to look a few things up for me—"

"Oh, now *he* was the one offering? It wasn't all your idea?"

"Well, no. That is, I said I was interested in a woman but was worried that she might be involved with someone, and he said he'd look into it. I told him not to dig too deep, that it wouldn't be right—"

"Even the little you did wasn't right." She'd remained standing this whole time. No way was she going to sit down next to him. Even having him in the same room was hard enough. Being less than a foot apart on the sofa? No way.

Lucas ran a hand through his hair and let out a sigh that was almost but not quite exasperated. "Margot, the stuff he looked up was the sorts of things that anyone spending a half hour on Google could have probably found."

Was that true? She really had no idea, as she certainly hadn't made a practice of looking herself up online. Angela once said that Damon seemed to have figured out a way to erase most traces of his personal information from search engines, including any photos, but Margot couldn't begin to determine how he'd managed such a thing. The former Wilcox *primus* had been very good at twisting magic to his own ends.

"That's not the *point*—" she began, but Lucas cut her off.

"What *is* the point, Margot?" He set down his mug of coffee without drinking any of it, then got to his feet. The living room was not very large, and he seemed to fill it as he stood there, staring down at her. "Do you want me to say it again? Okay, I screwed up. I screwed up because I had to know if I had even a hint of a chance with you. I screwed up because, once I'd seen you, I didn't even want to look at another woman. I screwed up because I'd spent my whole life thinking love was for someone else, not me, and then when I saw you at the gallery last spring, I knew I'd been wrong all along, and that it hadn't worked out for me before then because none of those other women were *you*."

During this speech, she could only stand there, feet seemingly glued to the floor. Damn it, he shouldn't be saying things like that. He should be protesting that it was no big deal, and that she was blowing everything out of proportion. She expected that sort of argument from him because it was the sort of thing Clay would have said.

But, as Lucas had already told her with some vehemence, he wasn't Clay McAllister.

"I—" Her throat felt parched, and she took a swallow of tea. "You expect me to believe that?"

His brows drew together, and she realized that had been exactly the wrong thing to say. Because he always seemed so easygoing, so unruffled, for some reason she'd thought he couldn't really get angry. Not that much, anyway. But in that moment, she realized he was very angry indeed. She wanted to take a step backward, but she wouldn't. This was her house, and she'd stand her ground.

"Yes, I do expect you to believe that, since I haven't lied to you about anything. I'd say that's a better track record than yours."

"What?" A flush of indignation swept over her, and she leaned down so she could put her tea on the coaster next to where Lucas' coffee sat. "I haven't lied to you about anything."

"Maybe not to me, but you've sure done a pretty good job of lying to yourself."

Oh, that was going too far. "I have not."

One eyebrow went up. "Really? So you haven't spent the past few days finding every excuse in the world why this thing between us couldn't possibly work, even when the truth of it was staring you right in the face?"

Her mouth opened to protest that remark, and then she shut it again. She was many things, but she hoped blindly obstinate wasn't one of them. And although she really didn't want to admit it, not to him, not to herself...he was right. Even when she'd been forced to acknowledge what her feelings for him meant, she hadn't wanted to accept them, had continued to tell herself it didn't matter what she felt for Lucas Wilcox, that she was an elder in her clan, and that meant she couldn't have any kind of life with him.

"No," she said at last. "You're right. I have been doing that. But only because I know it's the truth."

"I refuse to accept that." His hands knotted at his sides, and she could almost see the struggle in him, how he wanted to reach out to her but wouldn't do so unless he knew that such an overture would be accepted.

She let out a breath, drew another one in. "I can't change who I am, Lucas, no matter what I might feel for you. I knew I was accepting a lifelong responsibility when I became an elder. It's a responsibility that has to come before everything else."

Without blinking, he said, "Even love."

Oh, Goddess, why did it always have to hurt in the same spot, right there like a knife in her breast? Since she didn't trust herself to speak, Margot only nodded.

"You mean to say that not once in the entire history of your clan has anyone ever stepped down for any reason other than dying in harness?"

The words were said harshly, and she knew he'd done so on purpose, to try to shock her out of what he no doubt saw as blind acceptance. "Not that I know of, no," she replied.

"Well, that's bullshit. I mean, even the King of England once gave up his throne for the woman he loved, so I have a hard time believing that an elder of the McAllister clan can't do the same thing."

Although she didn't mean for them to, Margot's lips quirked. "Are you comparing me to Wallis Simpson?"

In answer, his eyes glinted with amusement. "Well, in this case, I'm probably the one playing the role of Wallis Simpson, but…."

Her feet began to move before the rest of her quite figured out what they were up to. But then she was standing near him, so close she could practically feel the heat of his body. "I don't know what to do," she said, and the voice didn't sound like hers, low, defeated. Where her anger had gone, she wasn't exactly sure. Maybe it had turned tail and fled when she finally acknowledged to herself that she really didn't have all that much to be angry about.

His arms went around her, and he pulled her close, his lips brushing the top of her head, his scent surrounding her. "It's all right," he murmured into her hair. "We'll figure it out."

How precisely they'd do that, he wasn't sure, but he'd also driven down here not knowing whether Margot would even speak to him, or whether she'd call down a posse of McAllister witches to drive him out of town altogether, and now she was letting him hold her, had seemed to have forgiven him. Miracles really could happen.

They ended up sitting on the couch, with her leaning her head on his shoulder. Something in her felt very tired, and he supposed he couldn't blame her for that. Wrestling with yourself had to be hard work. The box in his pocket was grinding into his hip, but he didn't care. He wouldn't have moved from where he now sat for all the world.

At length, though, Margot straightened up and reached for her mug of tea, which had to be mostly cold by now. Lucas had the feeling she'd done so out of reflex, or to give herself a reason to move away from him.

"I still don't know exactly what you expect me to do," she said.

There was the opening he'd hoped for. "Well, I suppose we'll need to talk to the other elders, let them know that they might want to start looking for a replacement."

That comment made her turn her head toward him and give him a sharp look. "Oh, really? *We're* going to talk to them?"

"I think that would be best. A united front, and everything." He paused and dug the box out of his pocket, opening it as he went on, "They might take the whole situation more seriously when they know how serious we are." Taking a breath, he said, "Margot Emory, will you marry me?"

Her response wasn't quite what he'd hoped for. Her eyes widened, and she said, "Are you out of your mind?"

No turning back now. He pulled the ring out of the box and held it up, pinched between his thumb and forefinger. "I could be out of my mind over you, Margot, but otherwise, I'm deadly serious. I've waited too long not to know what I want now. I want you to marry me and come live with me."

Silence. Her gaze flickered from the ring he held to his face and then back again. "Drop everything and come to Flagstaff with you."

"I don't expect you to drop everything. I don't expect you to get rid of this cottage, or never come back to Jerome. But I realized after you were gone how right it felt for you to be with me in my home, and I don't want it to be *my* home anymore...I want it to be *our* home."

She moistened her lips. When she opened her mouth to speak, he found himself not daring to breathe, not wanting to do anything that might upset the delicate connection between them.

"I—all right. That is, yes, Lucas Wilcox, I will marry you, even though I have no idea how we're ever going to make any of this work."

"We'll figure it out," he said, his blood seeming to flow normally again, even as he reached out and drew her toward him, kissed her, felt her mouth open to his, her exquisite taste stirring the heat within him once again.

"Wait," she protested, pushing him away slightly.

"What?" *Oh, God, please don't tell me she's changed her mind....*

She lifted her left hand, spread her fingers in front of him. "Does it look like it's missing something?"

Missing...oh. He took the ring, which had gotten mashed in his palm, and slipped it onto the third

finger of her left hand. It glittered there like a promise of better days. "Better?"

"Much," she said, cupping his face in her hands
and bringing him close so she could prove just how
much better it was.

CHAPTER FOURTEEN

LUCAS INSISTED ON GOING OUT TO CELEBRATE, DESPITE THE rain. So they climbed into his Porsche, and he took her to the top of the hill to the Asylum restaurant at the Grand Hotel, a place she'd been to maybe twice in her life, merely because it seemed like such a special occasion sort of venue. Then again, if this wasn't a special occasion, she didn't know what was.

The ring was a new and unexpected weight on her left hand. She couldn't help staring at it as Lucas ordered a bottle of what had to be an extravagantly expensive wine. When would he have even had time to buy an engagement ring? And how had he managed to choose one that was so perfect? It was large, but not so big anyone would think it was vulgar. But still, that had to be at least three carats of flawless emerald-cut diamond sitting on her finger, flanked on either side by a single baguette-cut stone. The metal was white, and could have been white gold, but she had a feeling it was platinum.

"How did you know?" she asked, after the waiter had gone to fetch the wine.

"Know what?"

"Exactly the right ring to get me."

He shrugged. "I saw it, and I thought it looked like you. I didn't think you'd want anything fussy."

No, she wouldn't. Fussy had never been her style. "And how did you know I'd say yes?"

"I didn't." He rested his hands on the tabletop and leaned forward slightly. "But I figured I'd better have the perfect ring if I was going to ask."

Some might call that hubris of the worst sort... Margot preferred to think of it as Lucas trusting in his very singular gift. "We still don't have any sort of game plan."

"We'll figure it out. I have an ace in the hole."

She raised an eyebrow, and he said,

"Trust me."

Normally that was the sort of thing which only served to irritate her. Now, though, she realized it was the simple truth. She really could trust Lucas, in a way she wasn't sure she'd ever trusted anyone else.

The waiter returned with the wine, removed the cork, then poured a sample for Lucas. He drank, then nodded, and the waiter tipped a decent measure into Margot's glass, then topped off Lucas' as well. They placed their orders before being left blessedly alone again.

"I feel so…conspicuous," she admitted.

"Why? Is the restaurant packed with McAllisters?"

A quick glance around told her that they were safely surrounded by civilians…tourists mainly, she guessed. "No. We're not much for fancy dining, luckily."

"Well, that's something I expect to change with you. I already have plans to take you to all my favorite places in Flagstaff, and we should nip out to Winslow to go to the Turquoise Room, maybe stay overnight so we don't have to drive home afterward…."

"Lucas," she said, and he stopped abruptly, looking a little sheepish.

"Sorry. It's just that I'd been hoping for a future I could plan for, but until earlier this evening, I wasn't sure it was really going to happen."

Something warm and happy seemed to grow somewhere in her breast. This wonderful man didn't want anything except the chance to be with her. What woman wouldn't be moved by such uncomplicated devotion? "Don't apologize. I want to do all those things with you, too. It's just—I guess I'm having a hard time seeing how we're going to get from here to there."

"We will." He reached out and laid a hand on hers, his thumb brushing over the smooth surface of the diamond and moving to stroke the skin along her finger. "In the meantime, we're going to have a great meal, and then...." Letting the words trail off, he gazed across the table, his dark eyes catching hers. Something in his stare made her shiver; she had a very good idea what he hoped would happen after that "and then."

She had to say, she was hoping for the same thing. Even so, she didn't think that precluded a bit of teasing. "Presuming a little much, weren't you, Mr. Wilcox?"

"Not presuming. Hoping."

What could she possibly say to that? Luckily, she didn't have to say anything, as the waiter came by with their salads at that point, and it seemed easier to turn her attention to her food. Lucas seemed to understand that she needed some time to gather herself, so he ate in silence for a few minutes. Then he said,

"When do you think would be a good time to talk to the other elders?"

Good question. Tomorrow was Friday, and after that it would be the weekend, never a good time for important clan business, as the town tended to get very busy with tourist traffic. And she couldn't imagine putting all this off until Monday. Better to get everything out in the open as quickly as possible so it could be dealt with equally as quickly.

"No time like the present," she replied. "Or at least as close to the present as we can get. Tomorrow afternoon, maybe? I'll have to check with Allegra and Bryce, but they're available most of the time."

Lucas appeared to make a few mental calculations. "That should work. Do you want to call them now?"

"Now?" she asked blankly, setting down her salad fork.

"Well, before they make other plans, or it gets too late...."

He really seemed to be pushing this, but okay. Might as well set things up now and not have to worry about it again...well, until the moment of the actual meeting arrived.

She reached into her purse, pulled out her phone, and put a call through to Allegra first. As she did so, the waiter came by and gave Margot an inquiring glance. She nodded at her empty salad plate, indicating that she was done, and he took it away, piling Lucas' plate on it with a clank that made her wince. Good thing the phone was still ringing and Allegra hadn't picked up yet.

But then she did answer. "Margot? What is it?"

No magic there...only caller I.D. "Hello, Allegra. Something's come up" —across the table, Lucas flashed a grin at Margot, and she sent him a quelling glance— "and I need to talk to you and Bryce tomorrow. Would two o'clock at my place work for you?"

"That would be fine for me, I think, and Bryce, too, I'm guessing." Curiosity sharpened her tone as she added, "What's this about, Margot?"

"We can talk about it tomorrow. Do you think you could call Bryce for me to confirm?"

"Of course. If he's not available, I'll let you know, but otherwise, we'll see you at your place at two."

"Perfect," Margot said, inwardly relieved that she wouldn't have to call Bryce as well. He'd be sure to ask more questions than she was willing to answer right now. "I'll see you then." She ended the call and shoved the phone back in her purse.

Lucas was watching her carefully. His expression was hard to read; the smile from a moment earlier was gone, and now he seemed almost thoughtful as he regarded her. "That wasn't too hard, was it?"

She shook her head. There was no point in telling him that the hard part was yet to come.

Maybe it had been, to use Margot's word, presumptuous of him to think he'd be staying when the last he'd seen of her, she'd stormed out of his house and made it clear she never wanted to speak to him again. But that sense of his had been tickling at the back of his thoughts, telling him he should probably pack an overnight bag, just in case, and so he'd followed his instincts and thrown the bag in the trunk of his car before heading down here to Jerome.

Now more than ever he was glad of this odd gift of his, the one that had always guided him to make the right choice. Because he could come back to Margot's house after a truly marvelous dinner and know he didn't have to go anywhere else.

Almost shyly she led him into her bedroom, which was less than half the size of his, but charming, with the dark wood trim around the window and the crown moldings and the blue and white quilt on the bed. "I hope your feet won't be hanging off the edge," she said.

He gave the bed a once-over. "It's a queen, right?"

She nodded.

"Then I'll fit."

Her eyebrows lifted slightly. "Oh, so you have plenty of experience with all the different bed sizes, then?"

"Some," he acknowledged. "Considering I always made sure to go to my dates' houses, rather than the reverse."

"What?" Her expression was a study in confusion. "You mean…."

He came to her then, took her hands in his. Her fingers were so delicate, so slender, so lovely…and none more so than the one that wore the ring he'd given her. "You're the first woman I've ever had come to my home. It was something I didn't want to share with anyone until I knew I was serious about her. Part of it was being careful, I guess—I mean, if you're seeing a civilian, you want to keep some things hidden until you're absolutely certain things are going to get serious, and none of those relationships ever did. Get serious, I mean."

"But you knew ours would be."

"I hoped it would." Lifting one hand to his lips, he pressed a kiss against her palm. "If it didn't work out with you, I knew it would never work out with anyone. So I took the chance."

"You know, your taking a chance is a little different from everyone else's."

"True." He fell silent then, seeming to consider her words. "I guess that was when it came to me. I have this talent, this gift, and yet I never had any luck in the one thing I wanted most, which was someone to love, to share my life with. But then I realized my gift was smarter than I was, since it was making sure I didn't make the wrong choice along the way. I had to wait, so the luck could bring you to me."

In response, she took his hand and cupped it against her face, then pulled him closer to her. "I love you, Lucas."

Something in the simple way she said those all-important words made the breath catch in his throat. He'd dreamed she might tell him that one day, but now that the moment was here, he couldn't believe it was real, that she did love him, and, even more miraculous, had agreed to become his wife. "I love you, too, Margot Emory."

She crushed her lips against his mouth then, tasting him, and then his hands were on her, undoing the ties of the wrap sweater she wore, feeling the silk of her skin beneath it. They fell onto the bed, which creaked faintly, and one by one the clothing they wore was tossed to the floor, until it was only the two of them, flesh to flesh, losing themselves in one another while the rain came down and the night became theirs, and theirs alone.

The next morning, Margot realized that probably the entire town of Jerome knew Lucas Wilcox had spent the night at her house. After all, it was pretty hard to hide a screaming-red Porsche, even on a rainy November evening. If she'd been thinking more clearly, she would have cast an illusion to hid the sports car, but she hadn't been thinking about much of anything except being with Lucas. Since she figured she had very little left to lose, she went out to breakfast with him at the Flatiron Grill, then brought him back to her place, even as they passed Tobias Miller on his way down to his studio. Clearly he had spent the night up at Rachel's, and so he just grinned at Margot and Lucas, said, "morning," and continued on his way. It took a good deal to ruffle Tobias.

The same couldn't be said about Bryce McAllister. Margot was definitely not looking forward to that confrontation, but the wheels had been set in motion, so there wasn't much she could do about it.

To distract herself, she'd shown Lucas around the garden, although November wasn't exactly the best time to show off its bounty. But it did have a spectacular view, and so they settled on the stone bench that had been placed near the edge of the property, just before it dropped down to the terraced beginning of the Willis homestead, which was immediately below hers.

The storm had disappeared with the night, and now only a few clouds lingered in a sky so blue it might have been carved from a single enormous sapphire. Margot could see the red rock cliffs of Sedona, and the San Francisco Peaks in Flagstaff, now crowned with white. For the first time in her life, she didn't feel a shiver of dread as she looked at those dark, dark mountains, but rather a thrill of anticipation. Soon they would be a part of her life, each and every day.

Lucas reached over and laid his hand on top of hers where it rested on the bench between them.

"It's a beautiful view. And we'll come back often to see it."

"I know we will. It's just…." Her gaze remained steady on those faraway mountaintops, on their promise of a life she never thought she'd be able to live. "Everything is going to change."

"Well, yes," he said reasonably. "But change is good. At least, that's what everyone tells me."

She couldn't help smiling, and shifted on the bench so she could lean over and kiss him on the cheek. "I think this is going to be a very good change. But it's still change, and that's something I haven't had much of in my life."

"You won't be going through it alone, though."

No, she wouldn't. She'd have Lucas at her side, and that thought was also both reassuring and unsettling. Her life hadn't given her much practice at being with a man. Yes, she'd been engaged to Clay, but they'd never actually lived together. Her mother still lived in the cottage back then, and Margot and Clay had begun planning to find their own place when she'd found herself unexpectedly asked to become an elder.

But she'd caught a glimpse of what it would be like to be with Lucas, and she thought she couldn't imagine a better way to live her life. It would be an adjustment, but it would be a good one.

His phone chimed, and he fished it out of his pocket and glanced at the screen. "I think we'd better go inside now."

"Is it two already?" she asked, puzzled. A quick glance at her watch told her they still had almost fifteen minutes until the fateful hour struck.

"No, but—you'll see." Smiling, he got up from the bench, then extended a hand to her. Still mystified, she took it and followed him along the gravel walkway to the back door.

Sure enough, as they entered the house, she heard the doorbell ring. Something in Lucas' sphinx-like expression told her he knew exactly who was at the front door, but he remained silent as she went and opened it.

Standing on the front porch were Connor and Angela. She looked so very pregnant that Margot wasn't sure how she'd made it up the steps, let alone climbed out of Connor's SUV, but it was definitely her.

Flicking a glance up at Lucas, Margot murmured, "Ace in the hole?"

"Precisely." His gaze moved to the young couple, who were standing there, staring at them expectantly. "I'm so glad you could make it down here. Come on in."

"Yes, please come in," Margot added, trying to push past her stupefaction and recall her manners.

She couldn't help asking, "Are you sure you're okay to be out and about, Angela?"

"I'm fine." Her hand went to the small of her back, and she added, "Well, mostly fine. I think I'll take a seat on that sofa, though."

She headed toward the couch and sank down onto it, Connor a step or two behind her.

"So what's this all about?" Margot asked.

Connor smiled, looking over at Lucas before returning his attention to her. "Oh, Lucas thought you could use some reinforcements. After all, this is McAllister family business, so the *prima* should be involved, don't you think?"

Well, that was true, she supposed. It was pretty clear what Angela's and Connor's opinion of her being with Lucas was, so throwing their support into the mix could only make this easier.

Or not. Bryce probably wouldn't much appreciate being ganged up on like this. There wasn't much she could do about it at this point.

So she asked the couple if they wanted anything to drink, water or tea or juice, and went to fetch them some water after they said that was all they really needed. It helped to have something to do, rather than sit there and watch the clock tick down to two o'clock.

And then it really was two, and a knock came at the door. By then everyone had relocated to the dining room, although Connor and Lucas had to bring in two chairs from the breakfast set in the kitchen, since the dining set only had four. Margot went to let in Allegra and Bryce, both of whom looked more than a little shocked to see Connor and Angela and Lucas there as well.

"What's this all about?" Bryce demanded, but Allegra gave an incongruous smile and said,

"Oh, I think I have an idea."

"You do?"

"Please, sit down," Margot put in hastily. "I didn't intend to spring all this on you, but…." She broke off, not sure of the best way to put it.

"But I thought I should be involved," Angela said calmly. "And before any of you say anything, I just want to remind you that this may be elder business, but the *prima* has the final decision."

"Decision about what?" Bryce asked. Margot could see him shoot a suspicious look in Lucas' direction; of everyone there, Lucas was the only one who'd remained standing, leaning against the wall behind her chair as if he hadn't a care in the world.

Now that the time had come, it was strange how easily the words left her lips. "I want to be released from my duties as elder."

"You *what?*"

Sitting next to Bryce, Allegra shot him a quelling glance. "I should think it's clear enough, Bryce.

Margot and Lucas Wilcox want a chance to be together."

"Preposterous," Bryce said at once. "An elder doesn't just up and abandon her duties because of a man…especially a Wilcox."

At that Connor raised an eyebrow, and Angela chuckled, although it sounded breathy, as if she barely had the energy to get out that much of a laugh. "Bryce, I think we're past the point where we need to be worrying about whether a man is a Wilcox or not. Anyway, Margot's given a good ten years of her life to this clan, and if she wants to be free to be with Lucas, then she should have that opportunity."

Hearing Angela speak, Margot felt a rush of gratitude toward the younger woman. She knew she and Angela hadn't always gotten along, but that didn't seem to matter now—the *prima* was doing what she thought best, no matter what their personal history might have been.

"Just like that?" Bryce said, clearly annoyed. "And who are we supposed to replace her with?"

"Boyd Willis and Henry Lynch are both very strong warlocks," Angela pointed out.

"Yes, dear," said Allegra, "but our tradition has always been to have two witches and one warlock as our elders."

That seemed to stump Angela, and she sent a beseeching look in Margot's direction. Margot nodded, then remarked, "That's true. I was actually going to suggest Tricia McAllister." Tricia was the most senior of their weather-workers, a talent that appeared in the clan with some regularity. Besides being a strong witch, she was married and settled, her son already relocated to Cottonwood to manage a restaurant there, her daughter starting junior college this year. Having their mother named elder shouldn't create a huge disruption in their household.

Allegra smiled her approval. "Yes, I think Tricia would do very well."

"Well, I don't," Bryce snapped. "What about all of Margot's illusions? Are we supposed to just go without them protecting us?"

"Of course not," Lucas said, speaking for the first time. "We've already discussed this and are ready to come down here once a week so she can continue to oversee them."

"I think that sounds like a great compromise." Angela paused for a second or two, her gaze roving over those assembled in the room, stopping at Bryce. He glared back at her, then seemed to subside, probably because he'd just realized that he was outnumbered on this one.

"I don't like it," he muttered.

"You don't have to like it," Angela retorted. "In fact, maybe it's time we revisit the whole idea of our elder system. Times have changed, and we should change, too. I think it might be better to have our elders only serve for four or five years, and then switch out. That way no one gets tired, and we have a chance to utilize a number of different talents and perspectives."

This announcement made Bryce's blue eyes almost pop out of his head, and Margot said quickly,

"Well, we don't have to decide that today."

"No," Angela replied. "But it's something to think about. In the meantime, Allegra, Bryce, you can approach Tricia and see if she's open to becoming an elder. If not, ask Henry or Boyd. But from this moment on, Margot, you're released from your duties." She let out a sigh and glanced up at Connor. "And I need to get myself back home. Doctor Ruiz would blow a gasket if she knew I came down here."

And there it was. Said so casually, but with a firmness no one there would gainsay. It was not the elders' place to contradict a decree from their *prima*. In that moment, Margot realized she was finally free.

No one lingered. Bryce and Allegra left almost immediately, Bryce still grumbling, Allegra looking remarkably unruffled. In fact, she even leaned close to Lucas as she left the house, whispered, "I was rooting for you two," and then was gone.

He and Margot saw Angela and Connor to their SUV. "Thank you, Angela," Lucas said. He felt as if he should say more, but he could tell they wanted to get on the road. Maybe the expression of gratitude on his face was enough. He had to hope it would be.

Then they were gone, and it was just him and Margot standing on the front porch of her little house. She was looking vaguely shell-shocked, and he slipped an arm around her waist.

"You all right?" he asked.

"Yes, I'm fine. Just…taking it all in." She leaned her head against his shoulder. "And Angela…I think I saw a little of Great-Aunt Ruby in her today."

"I take it that's a good thing."

"It's a wonderful thing. Ruby was a very great *prima*."

He tightened his hold around her waist. "So… what now?"

At first she didn't reply, only stood there, head still cradled on his shoulder. But then she straightened, pulling away from him slightly. "It's time for me to renew the illusions. I want to do that before I go. Will you come with me?"

"Of course." He'd wanted to see her at work, so he wouldn't turn down the chance now.

And so they walked the streets of Jerome, as she hid a gate here, or built a wall there, or made a street dead-end where it shouldn't. All so subtle, and yet so intricate, that he could only marvel at her talent, and at the strength of her ability to allow those illusions to keep going when she was nowhere around or even paying attention to them. What had she said? "Set it and forget it"? Pretty amazing.

Finally, though, she was done, and they went back to the house. She headed into her room and pulled a suitcase from under the bed. Without speaking, she began packing clothing into it, moving efficiently, as if she'd already thought ahead as to what she would take with her.

"Hey," he said. "You don't have to do that now if you don't want to. We can stay another night here."

"No," she replied, her voice firm. "I want to go. I'll have to come back and get another batch later, and decide how much I really need to take, but this will do me for a few days."

Lucas could tell then that she wanted to continue the momentum of the afternoon, to move ahead, and he certainly wasn't going to tell her no.

"Okay. Let's put that stuff in the trunk and get out of here."

The sun was just beginning to set behind Mingus Mountain as they headed out of Jerome, winding down 89A into the flats of the Verde Valley. For some reason, Margot felt as if she were leaving forever, but she knew that wasn't true—she would return in a week to renew the illusions. And when she came back, someone else would be elder in her place.

She'd thought that realization would cause a pang of regret, but it didn't. Instead, all she could feel was an overwhelming sense of relief. Was it true? Was she really engaged to Lucas Wilcox, and going to live in Flagstaff?

A glance over to where he sat in the driver's seat, handsome, reassuringly, solidly real, told her that did seem to be the simple truth. So much had happened, her brain wasn't done processing it. She hadn't called her mother to tell her she was engaged, or to tell her she was leaving Jerome, or—

"It's okay," Lucas said, and reached over to wrap his fingers around hers.

"What's okay?"

"*Everything* is going to be okay. I saw you over there, fretting about something or other. Whatever logistical knot you're working on, we can take care of it tomorrow. It'll be fine."

As he smiled at her, dark eyes glowing, she knew then that he was right.

It would be fine.

Everything would be fine.

www.ingramcontent.com/pod-product-compliance
Lightning Source LLC
Chambersburg PA
CBHW020245180626
46810CB00006B/2379